A roof under your feet

Also by Graham Lord:
Marshmallow Pie

A Roof
under your Feet

Graham Lord

028625 AF

Macdonald · London

First published in Great Britain in 1973 by
Macdonald and Company (Publishers) Limited,
St. Giles House, 49-50 Poland Street, London W.1.

ISBN 0 356 04544 7

Made and printed in Great Britain by
Redwood Press Limited
Trowbridge, Wiltshire

For Claude Mellor

1

He came on a quiet suburban afternoon in late September. The sky sagged with the knowledge of winter and at the corner of the street a solitary tree hunched itself against the breeze like a man resigned to middle age. A pair of birds loitered on the window-ledge of the corner house, discussing emigration. One of them heaved itself off the ledge and staggered up into the sky. Twice it circled the house, swooping low past the window. Then it turned and headed south. The other lifted a wing and inspected its stomach.

A bus rattled up to the stop. The passengers stared at the windows of the houses. 'Beckett Street,' said the conductor. The driver leaned over his wheel, chewing. The passengers stared at the tree. A woman looked out from one of the houses, excited by the noise. 'Come on, guv,' called the conductor. 'Beckett Street.'

A young man clattered down the steps from the upper deck. 'Sorry,' he said, reaching for a suitcase. Across the street an infant wailed, rocking the pram with amazement at the sound of its own voice. The conductor pressed the bell and the bus muttered away.

The young man hefted his suitcase down the street, peering at the numbers on the gates. A dog trotted happily across the road and followed him, grinning at his heels and sniffing his case. In the distance a telephone bell began to ring. The young man shifted the weight of the case to the other hand and the dog skipped about in surprise. Far down the street an old man shuffled towards him, bent over a basket of shopping. The dog darted into the street and savaged an empty cigarette packet. The young man stopped at the gate of number 57 and turned to face the dog. It watched him carefully.

'Thanks for the welcome,' he said. 'Be seeing you.'

The dog stood in the road and watched him close the gate and climb the steps to the front door. In the distance the telephone bell rang on, unanswered. The dog turned and ambled back, investigating the gutter.

From her window on the second floor Mrs Prendergast had watched the stranger stop, speak to the dog and come up the path. She crossed herself hurriedly and made a cup of tea.

In his room across the landing Godfrey Makepeace Thackeray stared hopefully at the sheet of paper in his typewriter.

In the basement flat Kasturbhai MacGregor remembered the last tenant and sighed. Her husband's daughter began to cry and Kasturbhai went into the bedroom to comfort the child. Its mother would soon be home.

8

2

The new tenant's first week passed undisturbed at 57 Beckett Street. His room on the ground floor was sufficiently furnished — a bed, some chairs, a table, a shelf, a gas ring and a fire, curtains, a mat, a chest of drawers, a cupboard. He made it his own with a landscape calendar and he populated the shelf with some paperback thrillers and four volumes of Churchill's *History of the English-Speaking Peoples.* The suitcase sat under the bed encouraging dust.

Each morning he woke late and lay in bed watching the autumn sun glint between the curtains against the wall. Occasionally the noises of the house would penetrate his room, the thump of feet on the staircase, the faint tapping of a typewriter, children's voices. Doors slammed, a bus rumbled by, and he would think of trains and queues and offices. He spent the days walking and drinking and listening in strange pubs. When it was sunny he would go to the park, sitting on benches and eating sandwiches out of paper bags.

In the evenings he stayed in his room and turned a

few pages of one of his paperbacks, reading some paragraphs several times, warming his shins in front of the gas fire. From the basement he could hear the lull and crescendo of television and the clatter of pans and the sounds of an evening family. Sitting low in his armchair he would stare undreaming at the fire. A floorboard above might creak and one night he imagined he could hear a bed being used for love and a child crying in the basement and from the landing the shuffle of running bath water. Each night he would fall asleep in his chair and the fire would starve from a famine of coins. He would wake shivering to the silence of the house and the howl of distant midnight cats soliciting dark comforts and he would massage his arms and brew a cup of coffee to take to bed.

One evening, walking home, he bought a newspaper. It speculated about the possibility of a new balance of payments crisis. He dropped it in a litter bin.

The girl rolled over onto her side and ran her finger down the man's nose. 'That was nice,' she said.

He grunted, and opened his eyes.

'There's a new lodger downstairs,' she said. 'I wonder what he's like?'

'We're all the same in the dark.'

'Silly.' She trickled her finger over his lips and chin and down his neck to his chest. 'You've got a one-track mind. I don't mean that. He seems quiet enough.'

'It's them you have to watch, Mongoose, the

quiet ones.'

'Mmmm.'

'Still waters, see.'

She played with his stomach. 'He's been here more than a week, now.'

'And a week yet, no doubt. And weeks more, and weeks.' He turned to meet her hand. 'Nice, was it?'

'Mmmm.'

'Move over, then. Move over.'

On the floor above them Godfrey Makepeace Thackeray jabbed at the keys of his typewriter. 'Chapter One,' he typed and sat back, tapping his fingernails against his teeth.

In her room across the landing Mrs. Prendergast sprinkled breadcrumbs on her window-ledge. 'Puss puss puss,' she whispered. 'Miaow. Miaow. Puss puss puss.'

Down in the basement flat Jawaharlal MacGregor sat watching the television set, chewing toast. His wife smoothed her sari, taking his plate and disappearing into the kitchen. The big negro woman looked across at him. 'Hey, mister,' she said. 'I need you bad tonight.'

He wiped his mouth. 'I am wanting only peace and quiet,' he said.

The woman pouted. 'I'm only human, man. We're only human, all of us.'

Jawaharlal MacGregor consulted the flickering screen. 'I am sometimes thinking I am becoming loving machine,' he announced.

His wife came back from the kitchen. 'The children

are all asleep,' she said. 'I am going to bed.' She nodded at the negress. 'It is her turn tonight.'

Jawaharlal said nothing and considered a commercial for a cheroot that guaranteed the attentions of blonde girls with shining teeth.

'God bless you, Kasturbhai,' said the negress. 'You are a good woman, I have always said.'

'Fair is fair,' said Kasturbhai MacGregor, hitching at her sari. 'It is your turn. Goodnight.'

Jawaharlal decided he disliked the man with the cheroot. The door closed. The negress moved heavily across the sofa and put her hand in his lap. 'Come on, mister,' she said. 'Do me a favour.'

Just above their heads the new tenant dozed in front of his fire.

3

It was the girl who met him first.

One evening she stepped off the bus on her way home from work and strode in a firm, emancipated fashion towards number 57 Beckett Street. Several of the passengers sat and enjoyed her legs as she walked along the pavement. Now that the girls had taken to wearing the 1930s look the sight of an old-fashioned thigh pleased them. She understood this and made the most of it. In the old days, when everyone had worn mini skirts, she had practised walking in front of her mirror, guarding against the critical wobble of flesh above the knee, afraid that her legs were too plump. But now it worried her no longer. In bus queues men positioned themselves carefully behind her, jostling close as she climbed the stairs to the top deck.

Now and then she was even followed home from the stop. Only once had this frightened her, when she had just managed to catch the last bus home after going to the cinema. It had been a slightly misty

13

winter night and a man had tracked her off the bus and along the pavement, the tap of his heels resolute against the damp concrete. She had refused to turn, quickening her pace and reaching the gate in a state of excitement as his footsteps approached. For a brief moment she had hesitated in the porch as she stood and faced the door of number 57, key in hand, dreading the squeak of the gate and the unknown roughness of his chin against her neck until he would walk away again as suddenly as he had come, unseen, into the fog. She had closed her eyes tightly, clutching the key. The stranger had walked on, past the gate, his tread muffled along the road towards another gate, another porch, another woman. She had stood there listening, heavily smelling the wispy night, her knees trembling. Such things do not happen in quiet suburban streets on winter nights. In her room she had shivered with relief and had not been able to sleep, her ears straining for the sound of his return. Later she had wept.

But on this autumn evening several passengers disembarked at Beckett Street, girls tired and pale from the jangle of the city and men with briefcases bracing themselves against the long tedium of the approaching night. At the gate she looked in at his ground-floor window and saw the new tenant's shadow moving against the curtains.

A few minutes later she knocked at his door. 'Hullo,' she said.

'Hullo.'

'I'm Georgia.'

'Hullo.'

She smiled and brushed a strand of hair from her eyes. He stood and watched her, one hand on the door.

'Georgia Shuttleworth. I live upstairs. In the room above you, actually.'

'Ah.'

She held out a cup. 'I was wondering. Have you got any sugar you could spare? I meant to get some at lunchtime but I forgot.'

'Of course.'

She followed him into the room. 'Just a spoonful would do. Well, a couple of spoonfuls.'

'I've got plenty.'

He seemed to have done nothing at all to the room since the last tenant moved out. 'I'll pay you back tomorrow.'

He was fumbling with the packet on the table. 'No hurry.' He held out his hand. 'Here.'

She passed him the cup. 'I don't usually run short. It's awful, really. I hope you don't think I'm always borrowing things off other people.'

'Of course not.' He poured a cone of sugar into the cup.

'You sure you can spare it?'

'Plenty.'

'It's awfully good of you.'

'Fine.'

She waited, the cup in her hand. 'I'm sorry to intrude like this.'

He folded the neck of the packet and tucked it between a jar of powdered coffee and a bottle of milk.

'I'll let you have it back first thing tomorrow evening, when I get back from work.'

'No hurry. Any time.'

'Well, I'd better be getting along.' She wrapped a second hand around the cup as though it were of value. 'It's awfully good of you.'

'Not at all.'

'Well, I'll be going now.'

He nodded. 'There's no hurry about the sugar. Don't worry about it.'

'Thanks awfully.' She walked to the door and turned, smiling. 'I'll be seeing you, then.'

'Right.'

'Thanks again.'

'Okay.'

'You've saved my life.'

When she had gone, moulding her buttocks with care as she climbed the stairs, he closed the door. He stood at the window and watched the night advance across the rooftops.

It was always best the second time. Georgia Shuttle-worth stirred and sighed, ruffling the man's hair. 'That was nice." she said.

'It always is. It's always bloody nice.'

'Mmmm.' She watched him as he lay with his eyes closed. She wondered briefly about growing old and moved closer to him. Georgie girl, he had once said, life is like a sewer — what you get out of it depends on what you put into it. It was probably not an original observation. Few of Owen's observations were original. She liked it all the same.

16

'He's strange,' she said, licking his ear.

'What?'

'The new tenant.'

'Oh, him.'

She measured his Adam's apple. 'I saw him today.'

'Oh yes.'

'I spoke to him. I was short of sugar. He's done nothing to the room at all.'

'Why should he?'

'Well, *something*. You'd have thought so, wouldn't you? It's like living in a tin of baked beans if you don't do *something.*'

He grunted and turned over on his side, away from her. 'Christ knows what you're on about,' he said.

She pressed herself against his back. 'He's shy. He wouldn't even tell me his name.'

'God Almighty, why should he?'

'I told him mine.'

'You bet.'

She pinched his back. 'Nasty.'

He shifted his legs to make himself more comfortable, settling down and breathing slowly. She moved herself against the base of his spine.

'Leave off,' he said.

She smiled in the dark. 'Tired?'

'Shattered.'

It was always better that way. Thank God for women's liberation. 'Goodnight, love,' she said.

Downstairs, below the level of the ground, Jawaharlal MacGregor slept deep. Beside him his wife Kasturbhai surveyed the ceiling, recalling Bombay and the letter

17

that had brought her to his side across half the world.

On the ground floor Errol Flynn Taylor, the sole fruit of a wartime passion in the back row of the Odeon, wrestled in sleep with the Playmate of the Month.

At the top of the house Godfrey Makepeace Thackeray dreamed of a world entirely furnished with bookshelves. He searched through thousands of volumes, flipping his fingers across their spines. None of the authors' names were known to him. He whimpered in his sleep.

Across the landing Mrs. Prendergast kept vigil in a high-backed chair by her window, the moonlight silver in her lap. She clutched a bundle of letters bound together with blue ribbon. She waited in silence and may even have been asleep.

4

The new tenant rose at noon and walked through the streets and the autumn park where the wind whispered of winter and the old men on the benches had rediscovered their overcoats. He sat for a while by the pond and watched the pigeons waddling self-confidently along the gravel paths. A man was launching a boat on the pond, his fingers gentle with love and the memory of yesterdays. Kneeling by the edge he coaxed it silently across the water, his thin coat straggling damp on the grass. It was a beautiful little boat with a proud, important hull and a gleeful way of running before the wind like a boisterous child. On the other side of the pond, on the grass, a young couple lay close together reviewing the future.

He lunched in a pub, feeding himself with bitter, cheese sandwiches and the warm mumble of voices and tinkle of glass. By now he was almost a regular. The barmaid smiled and smoothed her hands on her dress. The usual, love? Please. That'll set you up. Yes. Lovely.

He leaned on his elbow at one end of the bar and

19

listened.

'Just at that moment old Connolly comes prancing round the corner. "This is a respectable institution, Mr. Simpson," he says, "not a bordello." Silly old twit.'

'Same again?'

'There was this fantastic bird. He went straight up to her and said "Excuse me, miss, but haven't we . . ." '

'Make it doubles, Doris.'

'So I told him to get stuffed.'

'He was right! There it was, hanging out the window. Honestly, Pam, I felt so embarrassed.'

'And then this undertaker says "I'm only here for the bier." '

The barmaid was lifting his glass and rubbing the counter with a cloth. 'Penny for them,' she said.

'They're not worth it.'

She leaned on the counter. 'Dreaming, were you? Wish I could. Dream, I mean. Run you off your feet in here, they do. Still, I wouldn't have it any different. Keeps you busy. No time to mope.'

'No, that's best.'

'That's what I always say. Mind you, I like a nice dream. In the bath, specially. A good soak and a dream. That's lovely.'

'Doris!'

'Cor, here we go again.'

He carried his glass over to the fruit machine, rolling a coin down the slot and jerking the lever. Whirring, creaking, lights flashing. Click click click. Orange lemon grapes. This machine pays seventy per cent. Super jackpot. 'Everyone could see she was only

20

after his money. Poor old Tony.' He played and lost and finished the final pint.

'See you tomorrow, love?'

'Perhaps.'

'Bye, then.'

'Bye.'

The wind was cold on the corner of the street, slapping a poster against a hoarding. He buttoned his coat.

Georgia Shuttleworth measured out a cupful of sugar and carried it down and knocked on his door.

'Hullo,' he said.

'Hullo. I've brought the sugar.'

'Oh.' He stood with one hand on the doorknob. She offered the cup. 'There's no need, really. There was no hurry.'

'I like to pay people back.'

'Any time would have done.'

She flicked hair from her face. 'I don't like to forget.'

'Well.' He hesitated. 'Well, thank you.'

'Thank *you.*'

'Not at all.'

'It was very good of you.'

'Not at all.' He stood and looked at the sugar. Behind him the fire was on but he had been sitting in the dark.

'Well,' she said. 'I suppose I'd better be going.'

'Yes. Right.'

'Well, thanks again.'

'Don't mention it.'

She turned to go. He was already closing the door. 'Oh, by the way,' she said. 'We're going to the pub tonight. Owen and me, that is. Owen lives opposite me, on the first floor. We wondered if you'd like to come for a drink.'

'Well, that's awfully kind of you, but . . .'

'Please come.'

'Well, I . . .'

'Owen would love to meet you.'

'I don't . . .'

'It's silly living on top of one another and being strangers, don't you think?'

He was still hesitating. She glanced over his shoulder into the room, dark but for the feeble glow of the gas fire, the wall bare, the shelf hardly habited. Could he really prefer to live like that, with the makeshift impermanence of some stranger's tastes?

'Please. We'll pick you up on our way out, at about eight.'

'Well, all right. It's very kind of you.'

'Oh, good.' She smiled. Owen would take him out of himself. Owen was always very good with strangers. 'We'll see you later, then. About eight.'

'Right. Fine.'

'And thanks again. For the sugar, I mean.'

'Oh. Yes.'

'At eight, then.'

'Right. At eight.'

When she had gone he brooded in the darkness, remembering too much.

Owen Davies came in at 7.30 and kissed her, his

hands exploring her buttocks.

'I've asked him to come with us to the pub,' she said.

'You what?'

'The new tenant.'

'Oh, shit.'

She broke away from him. 'Don't use that word, Owen. You know I don't like it.'

She went across to the mirror and fiddled with her hair. He lay on the bed and watched her. 'What did you want to go and do that for?'

'He's shy. And lonely.'

'Oh, for God's sake.'

'It's only right.'

'We're not the bloody Salvation Army.'

'We're neighbours.'

'So's that batty old Mrs. Prendergast. So are the darkies downstairs. We going to ask them, too? Nice little party it'll make, and all. A handful of coons and a nut-case. Great evening.' She was brushing her hair, pretending to ignore him. 'You fancy him, is it?'

'I *beg* your pardon?'

'Him downstairs. Hot for him, are you?'

She brushed her hair energetically. 'Don't be so stupid, Owen. Really, it's time you grew up.'

'I know you, all right.'

'Now you're being childish. He's just lonely. You'll quite like him.'

Owen raised his eyes to the ceiling and sighed. 'Bloody hell,' he said.

Owen Davies was a Welshman who nevertheless

23

believed a valley to be no more than a ditch between a couple of mountains. His father had abandoned Cardiff just after the war in search of comfort and had discovered instead a bony laundress called Maureen. His influence over his children had rarely survived their christenings. Neither Owen nor Dai nor Gwynneth nor Llewellyn had even been moved to return to the land of their fathers. Their mother had always held strong views about Wales, partly because she had married a Welshman. 'Slag-heaps and sheep,' she had said. 'What sort of a place is that?' Their father had had to make his annual pilgrimage to Cardiff Arms Park alone. 'I'll not allow it,' his wife had said. 'I'm not having them there. It's bad enough the names you've given them without ruining their lives completely. God forgive me for letting you that night. I've always said Owen was born looking shifty and that's a fact.'

Allowing for his mother's weakness for exaggeration Owen Davies would nevertheless admit to himself on a bad day that his eyes were smaller and closer together than he would have liked. They might just have been passable on a small, thin man but Owen was unfortunately neither small nor thin. His body was broad, low-slung and somewhat inefficiently assembled. At school they had called him Hippo. Such circumstances, combined with the unhappy juxtaposition of his eyes, had encouraged him to assume a jovial and generous nature. In pubs he bought more than his fair share of drinks. Had his eyes been arranged more favourably Owen Davies would have been a richer but less popular man.

Although - or perhaps because - he had never been to Wales he worked diligently at his Welshness. He cultivated the Celtic corners of his nature, delving into Dylan Thomas and Brendan Behan and J.P. Donleavy in search of racial quirks he might be expected to exhibit. In the company of fully-subscribed Celts it could be heavy going. He had once accosted a man at a bar who was blocking his way to the counter. 'Look you, boyo,' Owen had said, 'could it be possible you are thinking of moving yourself, is it?' The fellow had turned out to be Welsh himself and accomplished in sarcasm.

But Owen was generally grateful for his paternal genes. They had bequeathed him a penetrating view of the world that he felt sure could never have come from his mother. 'Davies,' the careers master had said, 'have you ever thought of becoming a hypnotist?' Those bloody orbs again. But they could see, boyo, they could see good. They had observed Georgia Shuttleworth the day she had moved into number 57 Beckett Street and they had mesmerized her. 'You've got eyes like a snake,' she had told him later. 'And you're my mongoose,' he had said, helping himself to a handful of breast. Mongoose she had become.

He watched her now as she baited her lips in front of the mirror. He felt uneasy. It had been several months now. Was she getting restless? Sometimes she looked almost beautiful: a harsh, angry beauty when her hunger for him was strong; a drawn, used beauty when she lay asleep in the early light and he understood the possessive passion of men for haggard women whose only beauty is that they have borne their children and suffered their sufferings.

She was tilting her head to dab some scent behind her ear. 'Mongoose,' he said, 'let's stay in tonight.'

She turned and smiled. 'Silly.'

'No, let's. I don't feel like company.'

'But I've asked him now.'

'Well, cancel it. Make it tomorrow.'

She came over to the bed and bent and touched him on the brow. He could see she was a little excited. 'We don't go out all that much,' she said. He reached to pull her down with him but she stepped back. 'I'm all tidy,' she said.

She was reaching for her coat at the door.

'I love you, Mongoose,' he said.

'I know.'

'What d'you mean, you know?'

'I know, silly. Of course I know.'

'How? I've never told you before.'

'You didn't need to.'

'Hell, you arrogant bitch.'

She laughed. 'It's been plain for ages.'

Owen frowned. 'I've only just found out myself, see.'

She tugged the coat on and looked down at him with her hands in the pockets. 'You always were slow,' she said. 'Come on or we'll be late.'

He heaved himself off the bed and followed her out and down the stairs. Through the window on the landing he noticed that the night was dark and the moon was hidden behind a cloud.

The new tenant was waiting for them when they knocked at his door. She gave him a smile. 'Ready?'

'Yes.'

'This is Owen.'

The two men judged each other, uncertain, nodding.

'And you?' she said.

'Sorry?'

'You haven't told us your name yet.'

'Patrick,' he said. 'Patrick Kew.'

'P.Q.' She laughed softly. 'Nice to meet you, Patrick Kew.'

They followed her out and down the steps towards the pavement, falling in on either side of her. Owen wrapped an arm around her shoulders. The television blared from the basement, its glow bright against the window.

'The Lancelot Lounge tonight,' said Georgia.

'Oh Christ, no,' said Owen. 'It's got more poofs than a sultan's dinner party.'

'Nonsense. They're just artistic.'

'Artistic, is it? What's wrong with the Excalibur?'

'Eric.'

'He's all right.'

'He's disgusting.'

'He tells a good story, see.'

'He's revolting.'

They claimed a table in the Lancelot Lounge and Owen foraged, muttering, for drinks. The King Arthur offered plastic seats, taped music and lavatory doors marked *KNIGHTS* and *DAMSELS IN DISTRESS*.

'Nice, isn't it?' said Georgia. 'Owen hates sitting down at a table. He says a drink doesn't taste the same unless you're propped against the bar. He's a bit mad. He's Welsh, of course.'

'I see.'

He looked away, assessing the place. She smiled to herself. He was tense, a little afraid of her, not at all like Owen. He reminded her of Simon. God, that was long ago. She was seventeen and Simon had looked away from her just so. And then it had happened, one night in the coffee bar, he had looked at her, looked properly at her, and she had discovered him better than anyone since. He was only eighteen and already weary with an understanding of the world. Their friends around them had been loud, aggressive, and the music from the jukebox a throbbing extension of themselves. They had had no more than the hard slats of a bench in an empty bus shelter and twice the grass of a slope beneath a friendly bridge. He had gone the way of young men and she had never seen him again. At night she had cried for the terrible urgency of herself and the threat of womanhood. But she had always remembered.

She smiled at Patrick Kew. 'I'm sorry. I was dreaming. Come on, tell me about yourself.'

'Here's Owen,' he said.

5

Jawaharlal MacGregor pushed open the basement door. It was hardly ever locked except at night. During the day one of the women was usually in the flat, either Kasturbhai or Emily. Even if one of them had a temporary job the other would stay home to look after the children. This arrangement seemed to suit them both. Like any two women sharing the same kitchen they had their disagreements but he suspected that separately and secretly both Kasturbhai and Emily wondered why other women did not also share a man between them.

Jawaharlal could have answered the question. There were times when he pondered whether the world was mad. These did not recur very often as Jawaharlal MacGregor was not greatly given to deep thought, but occasionally he considered the possibility of universal insanity and now and then found the case proved. Once he had even seriously investigated the pros and cons of suicide but postponed firm action. Suicide, he realized, had about it an impressive finality that left little room for manoeuvre. One

29

could always commit suicide but one could hardly change one's mind about it later. Jawaharlal Mac-Gregor liked to keep his options open.

Firm decisions could get you into trouble. He realized that the great mistakes of his life had all been made when he had taken firm decisions. They had brought him to this basement flat with its two women, five children and 25-inch television set. There were times when he felt he ought to be grateful for possessing two women and a 25-inch television set. Not many men were quite so well-endowed. But such moments were rare and even at Christmas he found it difficult to feel much gratitude for the five children.

There had, of course, been a time when he had never made a firm decision in his life. Raised in the bosom of a large Indian family in Bombay - not to mention that of his young and sinuous aunt Gulab

Jawaharlal MacGregor's will had lain unemployed until his nineteenth birthday. That day, for reasons which now seemed obscure, he had announced to his family his intention of travelling to Scotland to claim his inheritance.

Jawaharlal's father, a merchant seaman by the name of Hamish MacGregor, had married Jawaharlal's mother in a brief ceremony in Bombay three months before Jawaharlal's birth and had then sailed away towards Glasgow and out of their lives. Jawaharlal's mother had never appeared to be unduly distressed by the disappearance of her husband but neither did she refuse to speak of him. When their child grew old enough to ask about his father she told him that he had been an admiral who had undoubtedly fallen foul of a German submarine.

Jawaharlal had always been impressed by reports of his father's opulence. Ageing witnesses mentioned a gold watch and the crate of high-quality whisky Hamish MacGregor had produced after the wedding ceremony. At school Jawaharlal encountered *Macbeth* and pondered the possibility that his father could be Thane of Glasgow and proprietor of several miles of Highland. On his nineteenth birthday he made his first decision. He would travel to Scotland to claim his inheritance. In vain did the family scold and scoff. In vain did his young and sinuous aunt Gulab weep and stroke his cheek. 'I am simply asking what is mine rightfully,' he insisted. 'I am then sending for you all and we are living in family castle in Glasgow.'

He had worked his way over to England and had tracked down his father's last known address at the shipping company's offices in the City. In Glasgow at last he had discovered his ancestral estates to be housed in a tenement building in the Gorbals.

The door had been opened by a little old man wearing a vest and sundry tattoos. 'Aye?'

'Hi,' Jawaharlal had said, beaming. The old man blinked and scratched his stomach. 'Am I having honour to be addressing Admiral MacGregor? Admiral Hamish MacGregor?'

The man had looked shifty. 'Whit is it? I'm no' buyin' no insurance.'

'I am Jawaharlal.'

'Oh, aye.'

'Honoured father! I am Jawaharlal MacGregor out of Bombay.'

31

Hamish MacGregor had suddenly understood. 'Awa' wi' ye,' he had whispered, closing the door.

'No, no,' Jawaharlal had cried. 'You are not understanding, Admiral.'

'Awa' wi' ye,' MacGregor had hissed, pushing the door to and turning the key.

'Admiral. I am coming from Bombay, sir. Ten thousand mile I am travelling. Is I, Jawaharlal MacGregor. Your son.'

The letter-box flapped open. 'For God's sake keep yer row doon.' Jawaharlal squatted to the level of the letter-box and peered in. 'Whit is it ye're wantin'?'

'Esteemed father . . .'

'For God's sake . . .'

'Ten thousand mile it is for claiming rights as son.'

His father hesitated. 'Whit aboot ten shullin's?'

'I am considering living MacGregor family castle.'

'A poond, then.'

'Honoured Admiral. Father. I am useful, sir. I am only wishing to be doing whatever you are saying, as loyal devoted son.'

'Bugger off then, there's a guid wee fellow.'

'I am not understanding, venerable sir.'

'Look.' MacGregor moved even closer to the inside of the letter-box. 'Look, I canna dae nuthin'. Yer mither wis a lang time ago. Tak' this poond and be off wi' ye.'

The pound note had passed through the letter-box. Jawaharlal MacGregor had stared in bewilderment at his heritage. 'You are wanting I should be going away?'

'Aye, I am that. Too tru'.'

He had perused in silence the paternal teeth glinting through the hole in the door. From Bombay to Glasgow for a Scots pound note. From the room beyond a woman's voice had called: 'Whit is it, Hamish? Whit's it aboot?' and Jawaharlal had understood at last.

At the bottom of the stairs three nine-year-old boys had gestured with broken milk bottles, relieving him of his wallet.

Jawaharlal stepped into the basement flat and shed his overcoat. On the sofa in front of the television set five brown infants crouched in a row, possessed by the vision of a boy yelling at his aunt about eggs.

'Hullo,' said Jawaharlal.'Hullo, my children.'

They studied the screen. Another child was chewing sweets and yelling at her mother. The mother was smiling indulgently. Jawaharlal Mac-Gregor was not a man of violence but he could not understand why the mother did not strike the child. He shook his head and walked through to the kitchen.

Kasturbhai was at the stove. 'You are back, then,' she said.

'I am back.'

Emily looked up from the dishes in the sink. She smiled at him over her shoulder, her hair hidden by a bandanna, her face blacker than ever in the corner. 'The hunter is home,' she said. 'Home from the hills.'

Jawaharlal smiled gratefully. He had always liked Emily. Even the English winter had never completely dimmed the warmth of her Jamaican smile. If only things had been different.

'Jagdish needs new shoes,' said Kasturbhai, stirring vigorously. 'He is having trouble at school with toes showing. And Rajiv is requiring discipline. You are too soft with him, Jawaharlal. There is apparently a dog with a tin tied to his tail and this is Rajiv's doing. There have been complaints from neighbours. You must speak to Rajiv. He is an hooligan.'

'He is only four.'

'He is becoming delinquent. You must discipline him.'

'Goddammit, he is only four.'

'Do not bring God into this discussion. This is not a matter for God.'

Jawaharlal muttered and withdrew. Kasturbhai had been the second firm decision of his life and the second big mistake.

There was a Western on the television and the children were biting their fingers. He had once tried to forbid them to watch Westerns because the Indians never won. It was no way to bring up Indian children, he had decided. It would give them complexes, always seeing the Indians being beaten. But Kasturbhai had overruled him. As a good Christian she saw cowboys as missionaries on horseback. 'They are spreading the Word,' she had announced.

'They are spreading bullets and racialism,' Jawaharlal had said. 'They are poisoning minds of our children.'

'You are preferring our children to wear feathers and warpaint? Is that it? You wish them to be dancing round totem poles?'

'I am simply pointing out difficulties. I am not

34

liking violence and racialism.'

'You are a heathen,' Kasturbhai had said firmly.

He slumped down in his chair and watched another redskin bite the dust.

Jawaharlal had drifted south again from Glasgow and had taken a job on the London Underground. He had made a few friends and less money. Life then was one room in Brixton and several thousand urgent tickets pressed daily into his hand at a barrier gate on the Bakerloo Line. At the end of each week he would spend the last of his few pounds getting drunk and buying himself a brief woman. It was the morning after one such night that Jawaharlal MacGregor had considered that his existence was unsatisfactory. He had been reading an American magazine that stressed the need for living a life that was meaningful and his own appeared to him to fall short of this desirable state. It was then that he decided to order a wife from Bombay by mail order catalogue.

Kasturbhai Bhave was no more than a name on the back of a blurred photograph but it was duly agreed in Bombay that she should join him in London and holy matrimony. Excited letters from home referred to proxy ceremonies and the bride's beauty. They spoke, too, of the difficulties of arranging for her immediate dispatch to England. None of this bothered Jawaharlal a great deal, for by now he had met and possessed Emily Jackson.

Emily appeared one day at his ticket barrier, magnificent in her generous Jamaican splendour and a London Transport uniform. She was large, soft, warm and extremely black. As Jawaharlal's best friend, Chandra, had pointed out: 'You have always been fancying a bit of black' and so it was. Jawaharlal MacGregor was weary of the sickly skins of the European women he had known and paid for and he was stunned by the heavy blackness of Emily Jackson. On that first day she had smiled at him and he had deduced immediately that Emily Jackson was meaningful. Her smile told of palm trees and hot white beaches and pale green lagoons and when she winked he could hear chickens squabbling in a dusty road and cicadas calling to the sharp, bright Caribbean moon. And as Chandra remarked before he learned to keep his thoughts to himself: 'My God, there is plenty good meat there. She would flatten a poor Hindu with her longings.' Within a few weeks Jawaharlal MacGregor was living with Emily Jackson.

On the television screen a pack of howling braves was setting fire to a homestead, galloping round in savage frenzy as a trembling white woman clutched a child to her breast. Jawaharlal stared and smiled. What a year it had been. They had wandered the streets of the city, exploring its curious ways and laughing at its solemnity. One perfect summer afternoon they had taken a train to Hampton Court and had felt each other by that curve of the river where surely King Henry and Anne Boleyn had also fumbled. Together they had licked icecreams on Hampstead Heath and hamburgers on Waterloo Bridge and at home, at night, she had fully fulfilled Chandra's prophecy with sturdy passion. Even her first pregnancy had made them happy. They had speculated

36

about the child. Would it have crinkly hair or straight? Fat, flat nose or pointed? Skin creamy brown or rich and black? They had laughed and poked their fingers at each other and Emily Jackson had begun to bulge and her solid body had seemed more beautiful than ever. And then, as they talked of marriage, the doorbell had rung and there on the step with a bundle in each hand was a woman from Bombay announcing herself to be Kasturbhai Mac-Gregor.

Jawaharlal had stood there contemplating the Indian lady and had turned to consider also Emily Jackson and the matter of her spreading belly. 'God in heaven,' he had said.

'How do you do?' Emily had said, smoothing her hands on her swollen front. 'Do please come in, Mrs. MacGregor. What a nice surprise. You are Jawaharlal's mother?'

'I am his wife.'

Emily had stared long and hard. 'His wife,' she had said. 'I see.' She had begun to laugh. 'His wife. Oh my, oh my. His wife.'

'And you, please?'

'I am his fiancée.'

'This I do not understand.'

'His fiancée. I am Jawaharlal's intended.'

'Madam. Emily. I am explaining everything.'

'How are you being his fiancée? I am his wife and coming all the way from Bombay.'

'Please, please. I am explaining it all.'

Kasturbhai had come in to perch upright on the edge of a chair and take tea. Emily, offensively great

37

with child, had sat opposite her and they had talked. Jawaharlal had sat between the two of them, silent and helpless as they set out to organize his life.

'It is obvious I cannot marry Jawaharlal when you are already his wife.'

'Also it is true you are having my husband's child. This is a problem.'

'It is sad it will now be a bastard, but probably not the first in the family.'

'We cannot now be turning you out.'

'You are a good woman, Mrs. MacGregor.'

'Please to call me Kasturbhai.'

'You are a very good woman, Kasturbhai. And my name is Emily.'

'You are an unfortunate woman, Emily, due to deceptions by my husband.'

'I don't think it was his fault.'

'Not his fault? He is married already and he is giving you a child.'

'I think perhaps he is a little simple.'

'Perhaps this is so. It is unfortunate.'

'I don't think he meant any harm, Kasturbhai. It was simply foolishness.'

'This is perhaps also true. It is a great sadness to me that you are in such condition because my husband is simple and foolish.'

'Goddammit,' Jawaharlal had remarked. 'Is possible I am invisible?'

'You keep out of this,' Emily had said.

'This is my house.'

She had pointed vigorously at her stomach. 'This is also yours, mister. And Mrs. MacGregor also.'

38

'Is possible I am throwing myself under first train tomorrow.'

'You do that, man. But first make sure of your life insurance. Enough for two wives.'

'Goddammit.'

'Otherwise shut yourself up.'

'You are changing, Emily. You are new woman.'

'Yes, yes. Lucky man, you, you now have two new women.'

'I think I am better going for walk.'

'You do that, only mind the traffic. You now have extra responsibilities.'

He had walked for miles and had wondered, muttering and swearing. At one point, trapped at the end of a cul-de-sac, he had struck his fist against a wall. When he had finally returned the women were sitting chatting amiably and drinking the celebration sherry he had been saving for Christmas. Emily was in a gay mood almost, he thought, on the verge of hysteria. She had every right to be, he could see that. It could not have been a happy experience for her to find his unexpected wife standing on the doorstep. It had not been much fun for him, either, but Jawaharlal could see that Emily had every right to be offended. Perhaps this wife, this stranger, could be persuaded to divorce him. That might be best. But whatever happened he could not part with Emily. Not for this unknown wife who was also somewhat ugly and looked nothing like her photograph. It was all most unfortunate.

He need not have troubled himself because the women had already devised a temporary solution. For the time being, at least until the child was born and things had settled down, Emily would stay. Kasturbhai as the lawful Mrs. MacGregor would also stay.

'And what about later?' Jawaharlal had asked Emily anxiously when his new wife had disappeared to bed. 'I am not living without you.'

'You now have a wife.'

'Is you are wife.'

'No, I am your mistress. I shall also be the mother of your child. But she is your wife.'

'You are not going.'

'We'll see.'

'I am not losing you, nor child.'

'Things will work out.'

'She is sleeping in bedroom?'

'Yes.'

'We are sleeping in here? On sofa?'

'I am sleeping in here on the sofa. *You* are sleeping in the bedroom.'

Jawaharlal had frowned. 'But she is in bedroom.'

'Of course she is in the bedroom. She is your wife.'

Enlightenment arrived at a leisurely pace. 'No, no. My God. No, I am not.'

'You have to get used to it.'

'I am not knowing her, goddammit.'

'She is your wife.'

'She is stranger.'

'It is your honeymoon.'

'You are making fun.'

'No, it's *you* who are making fun. With her. In the bedroom.' Emily had laughed. 'Tomorrow you won't be strangers any more.'

Jawaharlal had eyed her carefully. 'I am thinking you are mad,' he suggested eventually.

'No, I am sensible.'

'You are wanting me to be sleeping in there with that woman? You are positively taking delight in it?'

'She is your wife, mister. She has rights. She has come a long way for you.'

'I am not wanting it. In any case I am not liking her much.'

'This is no time to be choosy. You have duties to perform. She is expecting you to be nice to her. You have been married to her nearly a year already and she wants you.'

'And what about you? What are we to do?'

Emily had grinned. 'Perhaps when she is out shopping,' she had said.

Jawaharlal had stared at her. Then he had stood and walked away to share their bed with an unknown woman from Bombay.

The crack of gunshots from the TV jerked him out of his thoughts. A posse of yodelling white Christians galloped in dusty thunder after a straggle of terrified red heathen. On the sofa the children bounced and shrieked.

'Ride 'im, cowboy,' shouted Emily's six-year-old Simeon. 'Hit the trail, boy. Yahoo!'

'Injuns!' bellowed Kasturbhai's five-year-old Jagdish. 'Injuns!'

'Yippeee!' roared Kasturbhai's four-year-old Rajiv.

'Wa-wa-wa-wa-wa!' shrieked Emily's four-year-old Elizabeth.

'Bang bang bang,' bawled Kasturbhai's three-year-old Indira.

Jawaharlal watched them as they pounded the arms of the sofa and thumped their feet on the ground. 'Goddammit,' he said.

Later, when Kasturbhai had gone to bed and the house was silent, he looked across at Emily. She smiled lazily, warm and half asleep.

'I am thinking of first times together,' he said. 'They were best days.' She said nothing, but smiled again. He moved over to sit next to her and stroke her breast. 'You are my woman,' he said.

'I am one of your women.'

'You are best.'

'It isn't right for you to say that.'

'Is true, nevertheless. I am needing you now.'

She moved away. 'No, mister. Not tonight. It is her turn.'

'Goddammit, are you keeping calendar? Are you always writing lists in diaries?'

'We know.'

'Am I having no say in this matter?'

'You have duties and responsibilities, mister.'

'I am like bloody loving machine.'

'It would not be fair. Kasturbhai is a good woman. I am grateful even for half-share. She has never denied me.'

'*She* has never denied you? What is this she? Is it not I, Jawaharlal MacGregor, is providing nightly necessaries? Is it not I is exhausted by all this nuptial roundabout? Is it not mattering what are my prefer-
42

ences?'

Emily stood over him and smoothed the hair from his brow. 'Don't make it worse, Jawaharlal. Go to her.'

Later still, lying beside his sleeping wife, he regarded the ceiling and envied the new tenant. He was a man alone, a man at the controls of his own destiny. Perhaps he had no 25-inch television set but neither did he appear to have insufferable obligations and five children. Jawaharlal MacGregor rolled over and faced the wall.

In his room on the ground floor the new tenant was indeed alone. He sat gazing into the gas fire.

Across the hall Errol Flynn Taylor, propped on pillows, fingered a glossy photograph in *Playboy* magazine.

Above him Owen Davies and Georgia Shuttleworth lay close and weary, resting. 'Didn't say much in the pub, did he?' she said. 'Did you notice, we both talked and talked and he hardly said anything. What did you think of him?' But Owen was asleep. She closed her eyes and thought about the new tenant, examining the possibilities.

At the top of the house Godfrey Makepeace Thackeray tossed restlessly in his bed seeking in sleep some answer to the shortcomings of Chapter Two.

Across the landing, behind her bolted door, Mrs. Prendergast peeped from her window and watched a cloud move across the sky to dress the moon. 'Shall I go to him, Henry?' she whispered. 'Or will he come to me?' There was nobody there to reply.

6

Godfrey Makepeace Thackeray leaned back in his black-padded swivel chair in his room on the second floor and stared glumly at the paper that lay trapped in his smart new typewriter. The paper stared glumly back. 'Chapter Two,' it said morosely.

Godfrey Makepeace Thackeray eyed the page and took exception to it. It had torn untidily away from the pad, jagged at the top from a surfeit of gum. It had an offensive look about it, almost surly, as though it were contemptuous of his company. He rolled it out of the typewriter, crumpling it into a ball and tossing it into the wastepaper basket. It crackled there for a moment, expanding with a slight shrug, and settled down to die. Godfrey carefully tore another sheet from the pad and introduced it to the typewriter. 'Chapter Two,' it said and sat back to await developments.

The wastepaper basket was almost full. 'It's not fair,' he said aloud, and went to make a cup of coffee.

According to his birth certificate Godfrey Thackeray was fifty-two. This was strictly true. He

44

had, indeed, been born fifty-two years previously. But he considered himself to be no more than forty, an age that was ripe with maturity yet young enough for hope. Even at fifty-two Godfrey was an optimist. He had to be. He was writing his second novel.

His first had been a sudden, flurried affair. All his life he had envisaged himself as a spinner of words. 'Don't be absurd,' his wife had said. 'Come and mow the lawn.' One morning, however, his wife had failed to wake up. Godfrey had not disliked his wife and for several weeks he sympathized. But it was undoubtedly her failure to awake that morning that had brought him to authorship after so many years. She had left him several thousand of her father's pounds. Politely he had resigned his job at the bank, sold his house and moved for inspiration to London and number 57 Beckett Street. Less politely, but in vain, his wife's relatives had protested at his inheritance, speaking of lawyers and ingratitude. In two months, in the room on the second floor, he had written *His Own Sweet Will,* a short novel about a woman neglecting to wake up one morning and the effect this oversight was to have on her husband and relatives.

For this he had been rewarded with a cheque for £100, six fresh-smelling copies of the book and two inquiries from newspapers asking whether he was related to *the* Makepeace Thackeray. Foolishly Godfrey had denied any connection and later he regretted his honesty when he noticed how much interest there appeared to be in a descendant of Wordsworth named William. There was also the matter of Dickens' great-granddaughter Monica, whose writings seemed regularly to attract the attention of the gossip columnists. Godfrey decided that next time he would claim William Makepeace Thackeray as an ancestor.

His own novel had attracted a mere handful of reviews in the provincial papers and only one paragraph in a national. One of the heavy Sundays had observed that it was 'a significant study of the corruptibility of incorruption'. This had come as a surprise to Godfrey who had assumed it to be a study of a woman's failure to awake one morning and its effect on her husband and relatives. But he realized that the quote would look good on the jacket of his next book. His next book, however, was the problem. Once he had recovered from the excitement of searching newspapers for non-existent reviews and of failing to find copies of his book on sale he had settled down to produce the second. Since nobody appeared to have bought his significant novel he felt it was time to write a second book that was less significant but more profitable. He knew that this involved no more than coaxing it from the recesses of his mind. Skulking away in the grey jelly beneath his hair there lurked a best-seller needing only to be tempted out onto paper. But for three months now it had eluded him. It seemed to resent his efforts. Even worse, it appeared to be in cahoots not only with his smart new typewriter but even with the paper he had bought to receive it. He sometimes felt like asking it whose head it thought it was inhabiting, rent-free. It was, as he had pointed out, unfair.

Godfrey approached the typewriter again and warmed his fingers round the cup of coffee. He scrutinized the paper. 'Chapter Two,' it remarked, smugly.

He leaned over and reached for the file containing Chapter One and read it yet again. It told of the departure for London of a village nymphomaniac with long blonde hair, long slim legs and small pointed breasts that tilted upwards. When he had finished reading it he peered hopelessly at the page in the typewriter. It seemed to be grinning. 'Chapter Two,' it chortled. 'Chapter Two.'

'Write what you know about,' his publisher had instructed. Even Godfrey's optimism could not hide the fact that he had never in his fifty-two years encountered a nymphomaniac of any description let alone one possessing the requisite long blonde hair and long slim legs. Nor had he ever come across small pointed breasts that tilted upwards. What did one do with them? Did they behave in the same way as the ordinary sort? Godfrey had no idea.

He gazed for a long while out of the window, holding his manuscript in his hand. Then slowly and deliberately he tore it across and across and across again. 'Write what you know about,' his publisher had said. And what was that? Fifty-two years, one wife, no children, one legacy, one novel and assorted irate in-laws. Thirty years in a bank and a room now on the second floor of number 57 Beckett Street from which he had hardly moved for three months, three long months that now lounged in the wastepaper basket.

He collected his coat from the back of the door and walked down the two flights of stairs and out into the street and towards the pub on the corner. There, at an empty table beneath a sporting print, Godfrey Makepeace Thackeray proceeded to consume three unaccustomed double gins and three bottles of tonic water.

Lying in bed that night Godfrey wondered about the other tenants. In over a year he had discovered hardly anything about them. Those Indians in the basement, and the black woman. What was that all about? And they were called MacGregor. *Indians? MacGregor?* And that old Mrs. Prendergast across the landing. She never seemed to move. Who was she? *What* was she?

Godfrey slid out of bed, excited, stumbling over his clothes as he groped for the light. On the pad on his desk he scribbled a reminder for the morning, his writing large and unruly from the gin. Back in bed he nodded to himself and mumbled into the night. 'That's it.' he said. 'A party. That's it, a party.' In the darkness the room attempted to revolve around him.

Mrs Prendergast was the first to learn of Godrey Thackeray's party. It so happened that she was sizing up the space at the bottom of her door at the precise moment that the envelope was pushed through from the landing. For a while there was silence outside her door. Then footsteps receded down the stairs to the floor below. She claimed the envelope, her hand quivering. A card revealed that the pleasure of her company was requested on Wednesday evening by Godfrey Makepeace Thackeray, author of *His Own Sweet Will,* who would at 7.30

48

that evening be At Home across the landing.

She read the invitation four times, her glasses misting on her nose, and listened as he stopped at each door in the house delivering his announcement. She had known it would happen some time. This was Destiny. 'I knew it, Henry,' she said quietly. 'This is Fate, Henry. It is written.'

R.S.V.P., the card urged. Mrs. Prendergast sat at her little table and obliged.

Not long afterwards Kasturbhai MacGregor discoved her invitation lying on the mat inside the front door of the basement. It was addressed to J. MacGregor Esq. and His Ladies. 'R.S.V.P. is very good brandy,' said Jawaharlal when he arrived home and saw the card.

'You are ignorant,' announced his wife. 'R.S.V.P. is requesting a reply. Brandy is V.S.O.P. You are very uneducated.'

'Is what I am saying,' insisted Jawaharlal. 'R.S.V.P. is very high-class invitation. Is meaning very good brandy is on offer.'

'Now you are making excuses. You do not understand R.S.V.P. It requires a woman to tell you.'

'There are many things I am needing and it is not a woman.'

Kasturbhai sniffed. 'Some men are having a hundred wives. Some *men*, you understand.'

'Some men are also thrashing wives, which is not a bad thing.'

'God will protect me.'

'God is having troubles of his own.'

49

'There is no need to bring God into this discussion.'

Jawaharlal became excited. 'No need? Goddammit, woman, is you is bringing His Worship into discussion and all other discussion. God, God, God. I am wondering He is not sick and tired of you calling endlessly. You are never giving him moment to be putting up feet and watching telly.'

'This is blasphemy and I will hear no more.'

He left her in the kitchen humming *Rock of Ages.*

Emily was sitting with the children in the living room studying the cartoon strips in the evening paper.

'Hey, mister, are we going to the party?' she asked.

'We are going.'

He sat down in front of the television. Kasturbhai called through from the kitchen.'You will not be getting drunk again.'

'Goddammit,' muttered Jawaharlal.

'We are only going if you are not getting drunk again.'

'What is point of parties without getting drunk?'

'This is typical ignorant attitude. He is a distinguished man. He is author.'

'He is *saying* he is author.'

'No doubt he has proof.'

'I am not complaining so long as he is having whisky also.'

'Whisky is irrelevant. This is culture. You could be doing with spot of culture and we are going for culture and not for alcohol. Last time at Chandra's you were making a dreadful exhibition.'

Jawaharlal leaned over and turned up the sound on

the TV. In a row on the sofa the children watched, hunched, unaware of any drama beyond that on Channel 9. He looked at Emily. 'Is your turn tonight?'

She nodded.

'Thank God for that,' he said.

Godfrey Thackeray's invitation had a similarly disrupting effect on Owen Davies and Georgia Shuttleworth.

'We're not going, are we?' he said.

'Of course we're going.'

'For Christ's sake, why?'

'It's only friendly. We *are* neighbours.'

Owen clutched his brow with Celtic fervour. 'It's neighbours we've been for over a year now, look you, and not one finger have you lifted in the past to be friendly. What's so special now?'

'We've never been invited before.'

'So why now?'

She sighed. 'Because he's only just asked us now, that's why. You really are impossible sometimes, Owen.'

'Impossible, is it? It's me that's impossible, is it?'

'Now don't get all childish.'

'Childish now, is it?'

'Yes, childish.'

'Holy God, I never will understand women.'

She brushed hair from her face. 'No, probably not.'

He paused. 'What do you mean by that?'

'Nothing.'

'Go on, tell me. What was that supposed to mean?

Probably not, is it? What do you mean by that, then?'

'Let's forget it, Owen.'

'No, no. Let's not forget it. Let's get it straight. I know what you meant, see. I'll never understand you but that Patrick Kew will, is that it?'

She walked over to her cupboard for no apparent reason. 'Now you really are being childish.'

'In that case,' he said, 'you can bloody well get stuffed.'

After he had gone, slamming the door behind him, she sat on the bed and examined her motives. Then she locked the door. Later, when she was almost asleep, she heard Owen scrabbling at her door, whispering. She lay still and breathed heavily until he went away.

In the room below the new tenant was asleep. His invitation lay in the wastepaper basket.

7

Godfrey Thackeray was excited. They had all accepted except for the young fellow on the ground floor,
the new tenant. The room was tidier than it had been
for months and Godfrey had made it homely with a
bunch of carnations in a jar on the mantelpiece. He
had also invested in some extra glasses, a bottle of
whisky, a bottle of gin, a bottle of sherry and some
peanuts and cheese biscuits. He wondered why he had
never thought of it before. They said there was a
novel in everyone but of course not everyone knew
how to go about it. Well, Godfrey would do it for
them. The old house was creaking with material and
he had only just realized it. Beside himself there were
eight adults living at number 57 Beckett Street,
eight booksworth of raw experience in search of an
author. One of the women might even with luck turn
out to be the necessary nymphomaniac. For the sake
of his art Godfrey was prepared to do a bit of
research.

He flicked some dust from the bedside table and
turned off the main light, leaving the room cosy in

the glow of the anglepoise lamp. A momentary panic grabbed him as he thought of his room full of strangers. What would he say to them? Would they even have anything in common? He braced himself. Come, come, Godfrey, this is important. Save your sensitivity for the typewriter. It is a choice of boldness or back to the bank.

He wondered who would arrive first.

It was Mrs. Prendergast. At exactly 7.30 she tapped on his door.

'Mrs. Prendergast,' he said. 'How nice.' She was small and upright, dressed in an ancient suit that was now too large for her. She was wearing a faint touch of lipstick and a wisp of perfume. 'Do come in,' he said. 'Come over here and sit in the armchair.'

She poised herself with her hands in her lap, nodding now and then as he poured the sherry. 'What a nice idea,' she said.

'I beg your pardon?'

'What a nice idea to receive guests.'

'I did feel it was about time we got to know each other.'

'To *know* each other, Mr. Thackeray?'

'Yes.'

'You have other guests this evening, I hope?'

'Oh, yes. All the other tenants. All, that is . . .'

'Ah. For a moment I felt I might have been improper accepting your invitation.'

'Improper, Mrs. Prendergast?'

She raised her eyebrows. 'Indeed yes. If there had been no other guests it would have been quite
54

improper, would it not?'

'Oh, quite.' Good grief, he thought, she must be a couple of hundred years old, at least.

They sat and sipped sherry, she on the edge of the chair and he at the end of his bed. 'It is strange how impersonal a house like this can be,' he said. 'We all live on top of one another and rarely make any contact.'

'That is life, Mr Thackeray. We are as vessels on the open ocean ploughing against the tide in the darkness of night.'

'Ah.'

She pecked at her glass, firm and forward in the armchair, her thin legs pressed close together.

'You are a window, Mrs Prendergast?'

'These ten years.'

'I'm sorry.'

'There is no need for sorrow. My Henry has found happiness in the Great Beyond.'

'There is that, of course.'

'I shall join him before very long.'

'Oh, come, Mrs Prendergast. You seem very fit.'

'Death is impartial, Mr Thackeray.'

'Yes, of course.'

'My Henry and I will meet again before very long.'

'That must be very comforting for you.'

She smoothed her skirt. 'On the contrary, Mr Thackeray,' she said. 'I can imagine nothing I should like less.'

In the basement they sat and waited, the women fresh and crisp and Jawaharlal wearing a suit, his hair pressed flat with Brylcreem. The television set was switched off and the clock ticked loudly in the silence.

'Is time to be going,' he said.

Kasturbhai hitched at her sari. 'Not yet.'

'But is after 7.30,' insisted Jawaharlal. 'Is 7.35. Invitation mentioned 7.30.'

Kasturbhai sighed. 'You are extremely ignorant. It is not decent to arrive on time.'

'Punctuality is virtue.'

'Not for functions.'

'Supervisor is always telling me punctuality is virtue. I am five minutes late and he is saying punctuality is politeness of kings and mentioning some French monarch.'

'You are not a French monarch.'

'Is merely figure of speech. He is stressing importance of avoiding lateness.'

'And I am stressing importance of social rules.'

Jawaharlal frowned. 'Social rules? What are these social rules?'

'For functions it is not correct to be punctual.'

'Nonsense, woman.'

'It is important to arrive a quarter of an hour late.'

'Late? Why late?'

'These are simply social regulations. It allows host time to collect thoughts and arrange glasses.'

'But invitation is saying quite firmly 7.30. If host is wanting no guests until 7.45 why is he not putting 7.45 on invitation?'

'For good reason that then they would not arrive until 8 o'clock. Here is yet another example of

56

invincible ignorance.'

He appealed to Emily. 'Is this correct?'

She grinned. 'I think so.'

'To be late?'

'That's right, mister.'

He sank back into his chair. 'All whisky will be finished.' he muttered.

'Now you betray yourself,' said Kasturbhai. 'You are concerned not with punctuality but with drinking maximum whisky possible. I think this is perhaps typical.'

Jawaharlal grunted. They fidgeted and looked at the clock until it recorded 7.45. '*Now* is time enough,' said Kasturbhai.

He led the way. 'If whisky is all gone I am coming straight back,' he said.

'Sober,' said Kasturbhai, 'which would make a nice change.'

Georgia craned towards the mirror, rallying her eyelashes. Patrick would be there and she had chosen the brief cocktail dress with the cleavage. It never failed. Owen had once vowed that the way it cupped her buttocks would set a monk trembling.

That was the problem - Owen. She knew now that it must soon be over. She had begun to notice things - the way his stomach bulged over the top of his trousers, the pimples on the back of his neck, the irritating way he said 'boyo'. She still enjoyed the warmth of his body and the way he touched the back of her thighs. But was that enough? Very soon, she decided, she would have to end it completely.

She thought he sensed what was happening. He had encouraged her to talk about it and she knew he blamed it on the new tenant. But Patrick was just a symptom. He merely gave her another reason for breaking with Owen. She was not quite sure how it could be done. She had never liked partings, perhaps because change reminded her of decay. So long as life was stable it was easy to forget how swiftly it was spent. To end her affair with Owen would involve a double farewell, requiring as well an acknowledgement of the steady progression of days. She could not yet accomplish it alone. She needed help, a new target, another pair of arms to cushion her against the dwindling years. They would come and perhaps they would belong to Patrick and perhaps it would be tonight.

Owen walked in without knocking. 'Ready?'

She turned from the mirror, noticing how big and heavy he seemed. What had they called him at school? Hippo. 'Ready,' she said, standing and smoothing herself down. 'Do I look all right?'

He came across and stood close to her, breathing toothpaste. 'You look great. As always.'

She let him kiss her.

'I love you, Mongoose,' he said.

She broke away. 'Now look what you've done. Lipstick everywhere.'

He wiped his mouth, watching her tinkering with her face at the mirror. He could not pretend she was beautiful, not really beautiful. But there was something about the way she bent down to the mirror and widened her eyes. And that dress.

'You're gorgeous,' he said.

Her reflection looked up at him and smiled. 'Why, thank you, kind sir,' she said.

Godfrey Thackeray's party was in no hurry to warm up. The guests parked themselves in a polite circle round Mrs Prendergast's chair and prospected for common ground.

Owen Davies ventured to mention the landlord. 'Grasping devil hasn't been here in years,' he said.

'Oh yes, indeed,' said Jawaharlal. 'Goddammit, no.'

'The water-heater in the bathroom never works properly. Had to thump the thing yesterday, like. Quick upper-cut, see, followed by a left hook. Cried like a baby it did, hot tears on the porcelain. Rachmanism, that's what it is, see, Rachmanism.'

'Yes, yes,' said Jawaharlal. 'And we are having damp patches in basement like bloody great thunderclouds - excuse me ladies - big thunderclouds, goddammit. Please to give less water this time, Mr Thackeray sir.'

'We are lucky to have a roof at all,' remarked Kasturbhai. 'It is not always simple for such people as we to find accommodation.'

They shifted weight uneasily. Owen wondered how soon he could persuade Georgia to leave. She kept watching the door. Godfrey fussed round, pouring drinks and noticing that MacGregor was sinking the whisky at an alarming speed. At this rate he would have to slip out and buy another bottle.

'You are author I believe, Mr Thackeray?' said Kasturbhai. There was a murmur of sudden interest.

'Well, yes,' said Godfrey modestly. 'A novel, you know.'

'How interesting.'

'How interesting.'

Owen grunted.

'What it is about?' asked Emily. 'We shall all have to buy a copy.'

'Oh yes, yes. Indeed,' said Jawaharlal. 'Indubitably, Mr Thackeray. Please be giving less water this time.'

'I'm sure you're not really interested in my writing.'

'Oh, yes,' said Georgia. 'We always hear you typing away so busily. I've often wondered what you write.'

'Oh dear. I don't disturb you, do I?'

'Of course not.'

'No, no,' said Jawaharlal. 'This damn fine whisky. Yes. Not all.'

'Thank goodness for that. Well, if you're *really* interested . . .'

'Please tell all,' urged Kasturbhai. 'It is good to discover there is culture in this house. There is great shortage of culture these days, more is the pity.'

Owen sighed. Dear God, here comes the cuttings book. It's as bad as people with home movies. But at least it was breaking up the gathering. Georgia was looking over Mrs Prendergast's shoulder at a copy of the book, stiff and important in its shiny new jacket. Thackeray was exhibiting his newspaper cuttings to the MacGregor women. 'I think you must be very proud, Mr Thackeray,' Kasturbhai was saying. Jawaharlal himself was eyeing the whisky bottle.

Owen joined him near the window. 'You thinking

what I'm thinking, boyo?'

'Please?'

'The whisky. Not much left, is there?'

'Indeed no. We are perhaps becoming very thirsty soon.'

'Too true, boyo.'

'Please? I am not understanding. What is this boyo, please?'

Owen chuckled. 'Just a Welsh saying, boyo. I'm Welsh, see? From Wales, where men are men and the sheep are terrified. It's just a word of friendship, like mate.'

'Good, good,' said Jawaharlal. 'I am all for friendship. Boyo. Yes, friendship is good, boyo. I am correct?'

'Right.'

'We are perhaps shaking hands on friendship, yes?

'Yes.'

They shook hands.

'Right. Is bloody good. Now we are being friends, boyo, perhaps you are pouring more whisky.'

Owen glanced at Godfrey Thackeray. He was wallowing in female adulation. 'Might as well,' he said.

'Excellent,' said Jawaharlal, holding out his glass. 'Now wife is not watching please be giving neat double.'

Errol Flynn Taylor arrived with a heavy shine on his shoes. He stood in the doorway poking nervously at his glasses.

'Mr Taylor,' cried Godfrey, ushering him into the

61

room. 'How good of you to come. Do you know everyone? Mrs Prendergast, Miss Shuttleworth, Mrs MacGregor and - ah - Mrs MacGregor, and of course Mr MacGregor and finally Mr Davies.'

'Ah,' said Errol. 'Yes.' Owen had only met him a couple of times in the hall. Taylor lived on the ground floor, opposite Patrick whatsisname. A right twit he was, too, thought Owen, with his thin nose twitching and his eyes blinking like bloody beacons behind his specs. Godfrey was organizing his thirst at the desk.

'Is most embarrassing,' Jawaharlal was saying. 'Is most embarrassing introducing two Mrs MacGregor.'

'Sorry?'

'Bloody sorry. Sorry is correct. Yes, indeed so.'

'I don't follow, boyo.'

Jawaharlal leaned forward confidentially, gesturing with his glass. 'Him, Thackeray. Author. He is introducing two Mrs MacGregor. But is only one Mrs MacGregor.'

'One?'

'Other is Miss Jackson. Miss Emily Jackson. Black one.'

Owen stared at him politely.

'Is not wife,' hissed Jawaharlal. 'Eternal triangle, you are understanding. Goddammit, eternal is correct. Is going on now for hundreds of year.'

'I'm sorry, I . . .'

'I am telling,' insisted Jawaharlal vehemently. 'Ugly brown one is wife. Sexy big black one is only mistress.'

'Christ Almighty.'

'You got it. Christ Almighty is bloody right, boyo. Too true. Goddammit, where is damn whisky?'

Mrs Prendergast had begun to watch the door as though she were expecting someone. Owen was in a mood to notice these things. Georgia was doing it too and he knew why and girt himself about with the weapons of charm and wit and cunning that civilized men employ in battle. But what was with the old bird? Not her too, for God's sake. She looked about as sexual as a pad of blotting paper. Owen grinned. It'd be one in the chops for Georgia if old Mrs Prendergast got Patrick whatsisname instead. The Indian was burbling on about estates in Scotland. Two women, for God's sake. You wouldn't have thought the little fellow had it in him.

'No, I'm afraid Mr Kew's not coming,' Thackeray said.

'Not coming?' said Mrs Prendergast.

They all turned towards him the silence. 'I did ask him,' said Godfrey, 'but there was no reply.'

'Poor boy,' said Mrs Prendergast. They awaited further explanation but she said nothing. Owen glanced at Georgia.

'I thought he might like to meet us all,' explained Godfrey.

'Rude,' said Kasturbhai.

'I though he might be a little lonely,' elaborated Godfrey, louder.

'Very rude. It is not correct not answering invitations.'

Godfrey warmed up. 'You would have thought

63

he could at least have *answered*.'

'Inconsiderate,' protested Kasturbhai. 'Most ignorant and inconsiderate.'

Georgia said nothing, avoiding Owen's look. What was the matter with Patrick? Errol Taylor was watching her, too. He seemed a strange boy, jittery, and he stared at her with a nervous intensity. Owen was still looking. She smiled at him and walked across the room to talk to Errol. He shook her hand and prodded his spectacles back up his nose.

Owen grinned. Even Georgia could hardly go astray with Errol Taylor. He turned to Jawaharlal MacGregor. 'Have you heard the one about the rabbi and the Pakistani?' he said.

Mrs Prendergast left early and Godfrey took the chance to go out for another bottle of whisky. The way Davies and MacGregor were knocking it back the party needed extra supplies if it wasn't to dry up and crumble. Now that he had assembled them all it would be a pity to lose them again so quickly for the price of a bottle of Scotch.

So far he had been confined to the two MacGregor women. There *must* be a story there. Perhaps the husband would say something if he went on bashing the whisky. Godfrey resolved to pump him later – discreetly, of course.

There was also the girl Georgia Shuttleworth. Was she perhaps a nymphomaniac? It was obvious that she and Owen Davies passed more than the time of day together and yet when he had left the party she had been making eyes at the the thin fellow, Taylor, from

64

downstairs. Godfrey made a resolution to investigate the case of Georgia Shuttleworth.

As he approached the pub he quickened his step. He decided to buy two bottles of Scotch. He could always put them down as expenses against tax.

Errol Flynn Taylor listened to Georgia and tried to ignore the neck of her dress. He wondered how she would look in full frontal Hefnercolor across a glossy centre-spread. He swallowed hard and cleared his throat.

'Tell me about yourself,' she said.

He pondered her, blinking the sweat away from his eyes and sliding the spectacles back up his nose again. 'I'm a librarian,' he said.

She smiled. 'How marvellous. Do you enjoy it?'

How do you answer a girl like this? How do you tell her that you have yearned for her at the sound of her footsteps across the morning hall when all you could do was to sit on your bed behind the closed door with your fists clenched, dreaming dreams? How can you explain that you have known her in the night and buried yourself in her hair when you have never before shared more than a sentence together at the foot of the stairs?

'It must be fun. If you like books, that is.'

'Yes.'

'Do you? Like books?'

'Oh, yes.'

'Have you read his?'

'Mr Thackeray's?

'Yes.'

'No, we haven't got a copy.'

'Oh, I see.'

'I checked. When I got the invitation. We don't seem to have a copy.'

'What a pity.'

'Yes.'

She smiled again, twirling her glass in her hand. 'We should all read it, I suppose. I mean, since he's living here.'

'We should, really.'

She was looking over his shoulder, probably seeking Owen Davies. Errol knew about Owen Davies. He had seen him one morning with his hand on her hip and once at midnight Errol had loitered by the bathroom on her landing hoping she might come out and he had heard Owen Davies's voice from behind her door.

He licked his lips and swallowed. 'I could get you a copy, if you like.'

'Mmmm?'

'A copy of Mr Thackeray's book. I could get one.'

'Oh, could you?'

'Yes. Through the library, you know. They lend them from other branches. I could get one easily.'

'Please don't go to any trouble.'

'No, I could. Easily.'

'I don't read much, you know.'

'I'd like to read it myself.'

'I think we ought to. I mean, he is a neighbour.'

'Yes.'

'That's awfully kind of you.'

He did not know what else to say.

She put her hand on his elbow. 'I must just slip out for a moment,' she said. 'I'll see you later, Errol.'

He watched her go. She was stopped at the door by Owen Davies. They talked quietly for a moment and she left alone. Errol fingered his elbow and looked at the door. His face was hot and he had to push his glasses up his nose again. His throat was dry and he turned to find a drink. The two coloured women from the basement were watching him.

'What is it you do, Mr Taylor?' asked Kasturbhai.

'I'm a librarian.'

'My goodness. Do you hear that, Emily? Librarian. More culture.'

Jawaharlal and Owen Davies were laughing loudly together. *'Goddammit!'* said Jawaharlal, slapping his leg. 'Is good, that one, boyo.'

Kasturbhai clamped his lips. 'Time soon to be going. Jawaharlal is becoming tired.'

'So soon?' said Errol.

'Well, just one more. And you can be telling us about intellectual job stimulations.'

Emily yawned behind closed lips and wondered why there was no music. Perhaps she could soon go over and talk to Jawaharlal and his new friend without seeming rude. At least Mr Davies seemed to have some life in him. They were laughing together again. Emily liked to see Jawaharlal enjoying himself. She began to hum quietly to herself.

Georgia stopped in the hall outside the new tenant's

door and listened. There was silence. She wondered whether she ought to turn back. From high in the house she could hear laughter. Little Mr MacGregor was enjoying himself, anyway. It was funny how easily Owen got on with people.

She knocked on the door.

'Come in.'

She was startled, somehow expecting him to be out. She turned the handle and peered in. Kew was sitting in his chair in front of the fire. Otherwise the room was dark. She was briefly afraid. It was unnatural, almost ominous. 'Oh, you're in, then,' she said.

'Yes.'

'I thought you were out.'

He paused. 'But you knocked.'

'Yes.' She stood in the doorway, silhouetted against the light in the hall. 'Just on the off-chance. May I come in?'

He waved an arm. 'Be my guest.'

She closed the door and stood in the room. It was very dark now with the door closed. He still sat in his chair and stared into the fire. She shivered. 'It's hot in here,' she said.

She stepped closer. 'There's a party going on upstairs. Didn't you get an invitation?'

'Yes.'

'Aren't you coming?'

He sighed and shook his head at the fire, stretching his legs out towards its warmth. 'I'm no good at parties.'

'Nonsense.' She moved over and rested her hands

68

on the back of his armchair. 'It's not natural, sitting here on your own in the dark.'

He said nothing.

'Why don't you come and join us? Come on, Patrick. Please.'

He shifted his weight. 'There's no point.'

'Of course there is. Old Mr Thackeray's gone to a lot of trouble to be sociable. Can't you be sociable too?'

'Sociable,' he said.

She looked down in the light from the fire at the top of his head and found her fingers stroking the side of his face. 'Please come. For me.'

He sat for a while, unanswering, and she bent and kissed his ear.

'Georgia,' he said. 'I'm no good for you.'

She knelt in front of him, on the mat at his feet, looking up into his eyes. They shone with the reflection from the fire. He looked straight down at her and she knew it was all over now with Owen. His face was firm and rough, ugly from the red glow and the sharp shadow across his cheek.

'What is it?'

He shook his head, holding his hands along the arms of the chair.

'What is it, Patrick? What's the matter? Please tell me.'

'I'm no good for you, that's all.'

She smiled. 'Let me be the judge of that.'

He shook his head again. 'It'd be too late.'

She lay back on the mat and watched him, her skirt drawn high across her thighs. He closed his eyes.

'Come here,' she said, patting the mat beside her.

The gas hissed, the heat burning at her legs.

He stood up. 'Come on, then,' he said. 'I'll come to the party.'

He only stayed for half an hour, conscious of hostility. 'How *good* of you to come,' said Godfrey Thackeray, and turned away. The Indian woman sniffed.

Georgia introduced him to Errol Taylor, who nodded and stared at her and licked his lips. Kew fetched a drink and stood with Owen Davies and the Indian. The Indian's hair was growing wild by now and his eyes were bright. 'Goddammit,' he remarked, 'You are new tenant, boyo?'

'Yes.'

'Is bloody good to be meeting you. I am thinking we are now perhaps shaking hands. I am Jawaharlal MacGregor. If you are wishing you may be calling me Mac.'

'I'm Patrick.'

'Damn fine, Mr Patrick sir. You are knowing my Welsh boyo?'

'Yes. Hullo Owen.'

'You are knowing, then. Bloody good show. Now we are all boyos together. Damn fine.' Jawaharlal waved his glass. 'You are knowing wife?'

'No, I haven't had the pleasure.'

'Is no pleasure at all, I am telling you. Kasturbhai! Kasturbhai!'

'No, please. Don't trouble her now.'

'No, no, is no trouble. What is bloody woman for if

70

not to be entertaining friends? *Kasturbhai,* goddammit.'

She swivelled vigorously. 'Do you not see I am speaking with Mr Thackeray?'

'To hell with Mr Thackeray. Come and be meeting my friend.'

'This is no way to speak of host.'

'Come and be saying good evenings to my friend, Kasturbhai.'

'I am busy. It is inconsiderate to interrupt conversation.'

'Bugger conversation.'

Kasturbhai turned to Godfrey. 'I am mortified, Mr Thackeray. Unfortunately my husband is ignorant and of no culture. Please do continue.'

Jawaharlal focused on his glass. 'I am thinking I am beating that woman tonight,' he nodded sadly. 'Yes, is time she is beaten again. Is long time since last beating. Women are understanding no logic, only physical violence. Is true.'

'You could be right, bach,' said Owen. 'How's your glass?'

Kew stood and listened to them for a while but it all reminded him of too much, the banter, the jokes, the loud insistent voices. As soon as he could he thanked Godfrey Thackeray and took his leave.

'How *good* of you to come,' said Godfrey, and turned away.

By midnight they had all gone. Godfrey settled on his bed and assessed the debris.

Across the landing Mrs Prendergast sat and

conversed with her husband. 'He *will* come, Henry.' she said. 'I know it.'

On the ground floor Errol Taylor lay in his mauve pyjamas trying to concentrate on a copy of *Men Only*. He blinked and picked his nose.

In the basement Jawaharlal MacGregor was attempting to decipher his shoelaces. 'Goddammit,' he said.

'It is disgraceful,' said Kasturbhai. 'I am so ashamed I am speechless.'

Jawaharlal belched.

'Speechless,' she said firmly.

'Funny speechless,' he said. 'For woman struck dumb you having remarkable ability for conversation.'

'It is filth, your behaviour. Filth, you hear? You are drinking a whole bottle of whisky. There are stinks in here like a pigsty. Such behaviour is revolting. I do not know which way to look with you swilling away like a pig. What is Mr Thackeray thinking?'

'Goddam Mr Thackeray.'

'There again. Blasphemy. Have you no respect at all? Boozing and blasphemy and filthy jokes. You think no one is hearing? Everyone is hearing your filth with that Davies. And rudenesses with that ignorant new tenant. Loud jokes and laughing. How am I holding up my head again?'

'Try using neck.'

'It is no good joking. It is too late for jokes and filth. It is time for reckoning.'

Jawaharlal frowned at her. 'Enough,' he said.

'Enough? I am not starting yet . . .'

'I am saying *enough*.'

'Pooh. You are saying. *You* are saying. It is a miracle you are able to be saying anything considering the quantity whisky.'

'Considering quantity whisky I am considering quantity violence unless you are shutting up.'

'Violence? Violence? You are not capable to be killing ants.'

Jawaharlal wrestled with his shoe and fell back in the chair. He pointed at his foot. 'Please be helping,' he said.

Kasturbhai sneered. 'Thus we have proof.'

'I am asking assistance.'

'And I am refusing.'

'Then I am ordering, woman. Remove shoes double quick or I am finding shortage of patience.'

'You are finding nothing but a headache in the morning, which is an excellent lesson.'

'Remove shoes.'

'Remove shoes yourself. I am going to bed.'

'Remove shoes,' bawled Jawaharlal. 'Goddammit, you are wife.'

Kasturbhai stood in the doorway. 'It is time you were remembering it,' she said.

He stretched out on the sofa, his feet propped on the arm, and closed his eyes. He did not feel very well. He was vaguely aware of Emily pinching his cheek. 'Come on, mister,' she said. 'Give Emily a kiss.' But by then he was asleep and snoring.

On the first floor Georgia lay beside Owen and

thought of Patrick. 'He's lonely,' she had explained. 'He needs friends, that's all. That's why I went down. He shouldn't sit on his own all the time.'

'Friendship, is it?' Owen had said. He had used her roughly, as though his urgency could bind her to him.

There was a soft knock at the door.

'Ay, ay,' said Owen. 'I wonder who that might be?'

She pulled on her dressing-gown and went to open the door, instinctively tidying her hair. On the landing, in his dressing gown and carrying a bottle of whisky, stood Godfrey Thackeray.

He cleared his throat. 'Ah, Miss Shuttleworth. I was wondering whether you might care for a night-cap. I thought perhaps, as there's all this whisky left over – as I couldn't sleep, you see – and of course you can't drink on your own – well, would you?'

She tugged her dressing-gown about her and shook her head. 'Oh no, thank you, Mr Thackeray.'

'Godfrey, please.'

'Godfrey.'

'Just a quick one.'

'Oh, I couldn't. I've had too much already.'

'Ah.'

'Thank you, anyway.'

'Oh dear, what a pity.' He hesitated and looked over his shoulder.

'Well, goodnight,' she said. 'I must get back to bed.'

'Quite, quite.'

'It'll keep, anyway, won't it?'

'Keep?'

'The whisky.'

'Ah yes. The whisky. Yes, of course.'

'Well, goodnight then.'

She began to close the door. 'Miss Shuttleworth,' he said. 'Georgia . . .'

'Yes?'

He stopped. 'No matter. No, no matter. I'll say goodnight then.'

'Goodnight.'

She shut the door. From the bed there came a low chuckle. 'Dirty old devil,' said Owen.

A few minutes later, as they arranged themselves for sleep, there was another knock at the door. 'God alive,' said Owen. 'He's back again.'

She swung out of bed. Oh Patrick, Patrick.

It was Errol Taylor. He looked down at her bare feet and hoisted his glasses up his nose with his forefinger. 'Hullo,' he said.

'Errol! What's the matter?'

He would not look at her. 'Coffee?' he said.

'*Coffee?*'

He fiddled with the neck of his pyjamas. 'Couldn't sleep. Thought you might like some coffee.'

She leaned against the doorpost and folded her arms. 'Do you know what time it is?'

He blinked. 'Oh, is it late, then?'

'Late? It's after midnight. I was asleep.'

He looked miserable. 'I'm sorry.'

'I should hope so.'

He glanced quickly at her and saw she was smiling. His stomach lurched. 'You'll have some, then?'

'No, Errol, I will not have some.'

'I see.'

'It's time you were in bed.'

For a moment his courage surged within him, inspired and alcoholic. 'Yes,' he said. 'With you.' Then it retreated in panic, leaving him hot and dry.

There was a long silence. 'Go to bed, Errol,'she said at length, and shut the door.

Owen was sitting up in bed. 'My God,' he said. 'It's like a ruddy railway station in here.' She said nothing. 'Who'd have expected Errol Taylor?' he said. 'Of all people.'

She climbed back beside him. He began to sing, softly:

"Tramp, tramp, tramp, the boys are marching,
 Cheer up, Georgia, here they come
Ta-ra-ra-ra!"

She pulled the sheet up to her chin and clenched her fists under the bedclothes.

Owen Davies, jovial to the end, began to whistle. It was a popular tune, bouncy and built for brass bands. As he came to the last line she realized its title — 'Marching Through Georgia'.

She snapped on the bedside lamp and sat up, her face tight. 'Get out,' she said. He looked at her, startled, his lips still puckered. 'Get out,' she said again. 'You bastard.'

He could see she was serious. 'I'm sorry, Mongoose. I didn't mean anything, see.'

'Get out.'

He shrugged. 'Okay. See you in the morning.'

She said nothing, knowing that anything more would keep him from finally understanding. When

76

he had gone she knew it was for good, really for good this time. Tomorrow she would arrange for the lock on her door to be changed. She curled up and thought of Patrick Kew.

In the room below he, too, lay awake. Unable to sleep, he tried to persuade himself that nothing is inevitable.

8

For autumn the morning sun was warm as it splashed through the front windows of number 57 Beckett Street. It spread itself generously on the desk where Godfrey Thackeray communed with his typewriter and over the chair in which Mrs Prendergast sat looking down at the street. It peered into the rooms on the first floor, finding them empty. In the basement it stretched and yawned across the feet of Jawaharlal MacGregor as they dangled over the edge of the sofa. Only on the ground floor did it find itself refused admittance, rejected by the curtains drawn firmly across the new tenant's window.

Godfrey Thackeray addressed his typewriter with enthusiasm. Earlier he had briefly questioned the wisdom of his excursion the previous night to test the physical appetites of Georgia Shuttleworth. It was not entirely seemly that a man of his years should parade in his dressing-gown tempting a young girl with offers of midnight whisky. It could have been embarrassing. What if someone had seen him there on the landing? What if she had slapped his face or screamed for help? But such questions no longer bothered him. Neither of these things had happened and in any case a writer had to be prepared to take risks for the sake of his art. It was no good tucking yourself away in a garret or a rose-covered cottage in Cornwall. You had to get out and about, mucking in with the rest of them and quaffing deep of life's heady brew. Had Shakespeare issued his plays from a monastery? Had Dickens locked himself away with slippers, tea and muffins? They had not, and neither would Godfrey Makepeace Thackeray. At Georgia Shuttleworth's door the previous night their shades had stood at his elbow nodding their approval and waving ghostly flagons of mead and ale.

What was more, his little exercise had proved to be fruitful. A lesser man might have been affronted to be rejected in such a way, despite his obvious attractions and a bottle of whisky, but Godfrey felt no such shame. His quest had been not for bodily comforts but for knowledge, and he had found it. It was now quite obvious that he had been wrong about young Miss Shuttleworth. Far from exhibiting symptoms of nymphomania it was plain she was a virgin. She was undoubtedly pure and untouched. Had she not lowered her eyes and tugged her gown discreetly about her? Had she not resisted his blandishments? She had indeed. It was a lesson to Godfrey not to jump to hasty conclusions. He had assumed her liaison with the Welshman Davies to be of an illicit nature. Why? Because of circumstantial evidence, a look, a tone of voice. For a seeker after truth such evidence was simply not good enough. His research convinced him that Owen Davies had not obtained carnal knowledge of Georgia Shuttleworth and it had given him the idea for a story. He would write about a girl of purity and decency whom everyone mistakenly believed to be a nymphomaniac. A virginal heroine! It could revolutionize modern literature.

Godfrey Thackeray condensed his brow and jabbed at his machine. The words flowed rich and black against the white paper, chattering fast and double-spaced down the page. At his elbow Shakespeare and Dickens nodded at each other and grinned, thumbs up. Godfrey ignored them. There are times when a man just has to be alone.

Across the landing the sound of the typewriter jerked Mrs Prendergast out of her reverie. She had been gazing at the window directly opposite in the house across the road. It was a window of no extraordinary merit but it had in its time afforded her an outside interest. Flanked by striped curtains of doubtful taste it exhibited to one side a large parrot in a cage. The parrot spent much of its day staring across the street at Mrs Prendergast and she felt that they shared an unusual understanding. At times she had conducted experiments in telepathy with the parrot. On one memorable occasion she had silently urged it to turn the other way. After some delay the bird had done just that and Mrs Prendergast had recorded the phenomenon in a letter to the editor of *The Extra-Sensory Perception Gazette*. He had published the letter and had furnished her by way of payment with a postal order to the value of 37 new pence.

Since then she had kept him regularly informed of her progress with the parrot. She had recently discovered herself yawning every the time the bird yawned but the editor of *The Extra-Sensory Perception Gazette* had declined to publish further reports, explaining regretfully that pressure on space was particularly heavy due to the activities of poltergeists. During his lifetime Henry Prendergast had always been a man of mild disposition but there were nights now when his widow wished he would throw something about her room.

The tapping of Godfrey Thackeray's typewriter drew her out of her contemplation of the neighbourly parrot and reminded her of the previous evening. She had seen all her fellow tenants before but generally it had been a restricted view from her second-floor window as they came and went along the pavement. She knew, for instance, that the Indian MacGregor was developing a bald patch on the crown of his head. In close-up it was hardly detectable but from her perch at the top of the house it was as plain as a rocket base from a satellite. Perspective being what it is, Mrs Prendergast had always assumed the Jamaican woman from the basement to be short and fat and she had been slightly alarmed to discover her large and fat. But otherwise their meeting had been of no consequence. She had only accepted Mr Thackeray's invitation as an opportunity to encounter the new tenant, whom she knew had been foretold. 'It is Destiny,' she had informed the recumbent spirit of her dead husband. 'As you know, Henry, it is written.'

And then he had not come.

Mrs Prendergast had been disappointed but not unduly so. He would know the best time. Perhaps the stars were not propitious yet. But she knew he would come to her eventually and her life would be renewed. She knew it with complete certainty and now her days were filled with a patient hope. At the appointed hour he would knock at her door and deliver her salvation. She reached for the photograph album and turned the pages, remembering. Mother and Father, stern and faded in Victorian rectitude and second-hand clothes. Herself in frills on a pedestal, glancing at the camera with infant bewilderment. On and on, the pages witness to the years, to Henry in his wedding suit, stiff and terrified. She smiled and tickled her finger across his moustache. 'Jealous!' she said. 'You never were before. You never cared. Silly Henry. Naughty, *naughty* boy.' Then the record of deckchairs at Torquay, and Frinton, and the steep and narrow cobbled street in Marazion where he had slipped and sprained his ankle. And there was the bungalow where they had spent their twenty years and where he had said each morning 'Well, I'm off now' and every evening 'Well, I'm home again' until one night he had revealed his passion for a cleaning woman.

She lifted her eyes and mused across the road. The parrot mused back.

'Pretty Polly,' she said. 'Pretty, silly Polly. Naughty, *naughty* boy.'

Jawaharlal MacGregor bared one eye and perceived his wife standing over him. Her head was brightly wrapped in sunlight.

'Ha!' she said.

He closed his eye again and marvelled at the din it made.

'Ha!' she said, louder. 'So you awake. How is the feeling then this morning, I would like to know.'

Jawaharlal turned his head away and regretted it. 'Go away,' he said.

She appealed to the empty room. 'Go away, he decides. Go away. It is you who is having to go away. To work. It is now ten o'clock.'

'I am dying.'

'Good thing, too. Insurance will come in handy.'

'You will be sorry.'

'It is you will be sorry. Insurance now is a thousand pound. You are worth more dead than alive. There is much I could do with a thousand pound, so you be getting dead. We will not even need an undertaker. You have so much whisky in the body you are pickled already.'

Jawaharlal attempted to move his feet.

'Last spasms,' remarked Kasturbhai. 'Last sudden jerkings before rigging mortars.'

Jawaharlal discovered his shoes on the end of his legs. He held them up for a moment against the light and considered them.

'Yes,' said Kasturbhai. 'Legs stiff already. Rigging mortars always makes legs stiff. Then arms, then body. I am now calling the cemetery to book a grave. Or is it a funeral pyre on the banks of Thames you prefer?'

Jawaharlal opened both eyes slowly and felt

seedy. He swung his legs round and sat up, holding his head in his hands.

'The Lord be praised,' said Kasturbhai. 'Raising of the dead. Lazarus walks again.'

Jawaharlal scrutinized her. This was no time for domestic confusion. He smiled wanly. 'You are up early.'

Kasturbhai sniffed. 'It is ten o'clock. It is early bird that catches the worm.'

'I am not wanting worm. I am wanting black coffee.'

'You do not understand. It is I who is early bird, is you who is the worm.'

He took stock of her and felt inadequate. 'You are being very clever this morning,' he said. 'You have undoubted fine mind. I am understanding all this and appreciating sharpness of wit. Now I am asking coffee.'

Kasturbhai rested on her broom and observed him. 'You may be asking coffee till the cows come home,' she said.

'I am not expecting cows, only coffee.'

'And I am expecting apology.'

'Apology?'

'Apology.'

'I am not understanding.'

'Indeed you are understanding. You are a stubborn man.'

'Please be explaining.'

She turned away and busied herself with the broom, poking between his feet at specks of dust. 'I have no time for explaining,' she said briskly. 'I have no time for lying around the sofa all day until ten o'clock and losing job and sending wife and children onto the streets to beg bread. If you do not remember disgrace and filth of last night whisky I have no time for reminding you, nor of conversations on filthy topics. If you do not remember any of that and embarrassing me in front of neighbours and threatening violence then I am sorry for you, Jawaharlal MacGregor.'

'Filth?'

'Filth. Disgusting conversations and behaviour.'

'I am not remembering.'

'And I do not remember how to make coffee.'

She dusted the top of the television set and mantelpiece and plumped up the cushions in the armchair. He watched and felt old and tired.

'And blasphemy,' she said. 'You are of evil tongue and much given to blasphemy.'

He felt his temples with the tips of his fingers. At times the world was not a friendly place.

'I am sorry,' he announced.

She paused fractionally in her progress across the room. 'For what is it you are sorry?' she asked, polishing vigorously.

He held his head together with his hands. 'I am sorry for spectacle last night.'

'And whisky?'

'And whisky.'

'And blasphemy?'

'And blasphemy.'

'And offering violence?'

'Goddammit in hell!'

'Yes?'

Jawaharlal clenched his eyes. 'And offering violence,' he muttered.

'I should think so, too.'

'Now where is damn coffee?'

She was working strenuously on an ornament at the table by the window. 'In kitchen,' she said. 'I made it ten minutes ago. You are better drinking it quick before it is cold.'

Three miles away Errol Flynn Taylor was arranging with a nearby library to collect a copy of *His Own Sweet Will* by Godfrey Makepeace Thackeray. Four miles away Emily Jackson stood by a ticket barrier feeling queasy and vaguely discontented. Ten miles away Owen Davies sat at a desk in an office feeling less queasy but more discontented. In a different part of the city Georgia Shuttleworth was just reaching for the telephone to request a locksmith to rearrange her life. As she did so she thought of Patrick Kew. He, by coincidence, was not thinking of her at all but was lying in bed trying to decide whether to roll over and go back to sleep.

9

Errol Taylor rode home from the library by bus, examining on the top deck the novel by Godfrey Makepeace Thackeray. He realized now why he had had such difficulty tracking down a copy. Not only was it published by a small and not very reputable firm but it was also rather bad. *'TO MY MUSE'* it promised on the dedication page, announcing further that it took its title from a quotation from Wordsworth's *'Upon Westminster Bridge'*:

Ne'er saw I, never felt, a calm so deep!
The river glideth at his own sweet will.

Errol Flynn Taylor did not go much for that sort of thing. For a start he did not go much for William Wordsworth. The thought of all those long nature rambles left him feeling weak. Errol was a city lad who would have derived little pleasure from suddenly encountering a host of ten thousand jocund golden daffodils tossing their heads in sprightly dance. He had read with approval a recent criticism of Wordsworth's claim to have wandered about lonely as a cloud which had pointed out that clouds in the Lake District are rarely lonely, tending rather to travel together in solid convoy. As a man who walked with his eyes on the pavement Errol knew little of the habits of clouds and even less about the Lake District but he felt Wordsworth had been rightly put in his place.

Not that he had anything against poets as such. He was, in fact, in his own small way, a poet himself. A recent tranquil recollection of his own, composed in midnight solitude, read:

Crouching
On the couch
A scratching
At the catch
And clutching
Crutchwise

It was entitled *'Destiny'* and Errol was rather pleased with it. It was a darned sight better that Wordsworth, anyway.

On the back flap of the book's jacket Godfrey Makepeace Thackeray smiled uncertainly out at the world. He had, the blurb announced, come late to Literature, being a man of mature years. This, however, was a point in his favour since it guaranteed the reader a work of thoughtful, well-considered gestation. The author was a remarkable and exciting discovery with a style of stunning originality and a vision of searing breadth and clarity. 'The reader,' the blurb concluded, 'should not be deluded by the simplicity of the novel into believing it to be simplistic. For by its very simplicity this brilliant first novel achieves a complex examination of the human predicament. It is a devastating debut.'

A large woman with a shopping basket wedged herself into the seat next to him, jamming Errol up against the window. He wiped his nose with the back of his hand and wondered how many devastating debuts he had witnessed in five years as a librarian. He had developed a definite dislike for authors. It was not that he was jealous of them. There was no longer any kudos in being a writer, let alone any money. No, what annoyed him was that they wrote at all. Who wanted their miserable words? Not the public, that was for sure, and certainly not the librarians. No sooner were their books all catalogued and sorted out than a whole new batch would arrive and mess everything up all over again. It reminded Errol of Monday mornings when he was forced to watch, helpless, as the magnificent symmetry of his shelves and catalogues was vandalized by people coming in and borrowing books. For Errol a library was a thing of beauty in itself, a communion of mathematics and art. Too many people saw it merely as a convenience, and a public one at that.

He read the first few paragraphs of Godfrey Thackeray's novel. It was terrible — not just all right or slightly below par but completely appalling. The man appeared to be illiterate. And yet Errol was grateful to him. But for his party he would never have met Georgia. But for his book he would not have had an excuse to see her again.

Thinking of Georgia sent his glasses sliding down

his nose. She was not, of course, the first. In his late teens he had taken certain liberties with Doris from the bakery and Rene from Woolworths and Maisie from up the gasworks. None of them, however, had returned for second helpings and apart from brief encounters in doorways with Sylv from Marks and Sparks and Doreen from Knott, Knight and Tompkins, Errol's twenties had so far proved loveless. This was partly because he never seemed to meet any girls who might have qualified for the shiny pages of *Playboy* and it was *Playboy* that influenced his tastes. But he also understood vaguely that women did not fall over themselves to get at him. He knew it, but did not know why. He bathed every week and brushed his teeth each night. He had no nasty habits of which he was aware. He was intelligent — yes, he was sure he was intelligent. So why was there this problem with women?

He knew he was shy but that was supposed to be an attraction. It made you appear aloof and interesting, as though you were much occupied with great thoughts. And he was just as keen as anyone else. Errol wiped his nose again with the back of his hand. Was he repulsive? Did he have personal odours? God help him, was he perhaps queer?

These and other quetions occupied him until his bus arrived at the stop in Beckett Street. He alighted and walked nervously towards number 57, clutching Godfrey Thackeray's masterpiece under his arm.

An hour later, bathed, shaved, freshly dressed and carefully annointed with Ruffian, the Rugged Lotion For Masculine Men, Errol Flynn Taylor sat on his bed and awaited the return of Georgia Shuttleworth.

Georgia was also much on the mind of Owen Davies as he swayed homewards several yards beneath the city streets, grasping a hand-strap and examining the hairs on the back of the neck of the man in front.

Owen generally tried to avoid the rush hour by stopping off on his way home for a couple of pints in the Plough and Gosling. It was a warm and unpretentious pub with a warm and unpretentious landlord and an equally warm and unpretentious barmaid called Polly. Lewd regulars called her Suki on account of the nursery rhyme about kettles, but she was a kindly lady who had on occasion provided Owen with consolation during previous tiffs with Georgia. But on this particular evening Owen found himself walking away from Polly and the Plough and Gosling and catching an early train home. Something told him that the Georgia situation was developing into more than a tiff. Some deep Celtic instinct warned him to hurry back to Beckett Street, preferably bearing a box of chocolates. He had not felt so uneasy since the morning his father prepared to thrash him in the presence of a police constable for selling flowers he had stolen off the graves in the local cemetery.

It was not a pleasant journey. From jammed tube to crowded bus Owen Davies fought for his inalienable right as a British subject to return home sound of mind and body. He was not in a sweet mood as he climbed the stairs to the first floor. A suspicious-looking man in white overalls and carrying a box was closing Georgia's door.

91

Owen approached him low, square and righteous, the box of chocolates under his arm.

'Ta all the same, mate, but I never use 'em. Fags is my vice. Fags an' bitter.'

'What the hell are you talking about?'

The man grinned. 'Them chocs. Lovely thought an' all, but no, ta.'

'Who are you, boyo?'

The intruder clicked the door shut and pushed it, testing the lock. 'Fred Hughes, mate, that's me. Corst me friends call me Fingers.'

'Fingers?'

'Fingers ain't wot they Hughes ter be. Ho, ho. Get it? Look. Fingers . . .'

Owen came straight to the point. 'Come on then, boyo. What have you nicked?'

Fingers Hughes was affronted. '*Nicked?* Wot yer fink I am, a leaf? That's a right liberty. That's slander, mate, that's wot it is. Slander.'

'Come on, then. Empty them.'

'Empty them?'

'Your pockets, see.'

Frederick Hughes, known to his friends as Fingers, wagged one of them under Owen Davies' nose. 'Now look 'ere, yer steamin' great Welsh git. Yer cast any more aspersions, mate, and I'll 'ave yer by the short and curlies. Who d'yer fink you are, anyway?'

'I am the fiancé of the lady whose room you have just burgled, see.'

Fingers Hughes regarded Owen Davies long and hard and with growing mirth and the arrival of understanding. 'The lady's fiasco, eh? Gaw blimey.

92

Not fer much longer you're not, mate.'

Owen blinked. 'What d'you mean?'

Fingers Hughes grinned and tapped the side of his nose confidentially. 'I won't tell no one, mate, but I've just changed the lady's lock. Instructions. Urgent, too, she said. Pay double, she said, and me on overtime an' all. Her fiasco! Gawd Almighty, that's rich, that is. Wotcher bin up to then, mate? Bin overdoin' the conjugal demands then, eh?'

Owen checked the lock in Georgia's door. It regarded him thinly, shiny and new.

Fingers Hughes wiped his palms on his overalls and picked up his tool box. 'Well, I'll be off, then. Get 'ome fer me tea.'

'A new lock.'

'No 'ard feelin's, mate. I can understand yer apprehensions, like. No 'ard feelin's, as the bishop said to the actress.' He began to negotiate the stairs.

'Hold on,' said Owen. 'Mr Hughes. I'm sorry. It was a genuine mistake, see.'

'Not to worry, mate. Could 'appen to any of us.'

'Look. Could you let me have a key to fit the new lock? I'll pay, of course.'

Fingers Hughes shook his head sadly. 'Nah. Nah, wouldn't be effical, would it, like? Wouldn't be effical at all.'

'A quid, then.'

'Cor, yer fancy this bird an' all, don't yer?'

'I'm going to marry her, see.'

'Yus, well. She'll likely give you a spare anyway, then, won't she?'

'Two quid. Come on, bach. Two quid.'

Fingers Hughes stood on the stairs and contemplated the accumulation of such riches. Then he shook his head. 'Corst, it's temptin',' he said. 'I'm not denyin' that. It's temptin', all right. But it wouldn't be right, like, would it? Not strictly speakin', if yer see what I mean. It'd be a breach of faith, wouldn't it? Yer locksmith's like yer priest, like yer doctor. Prefessional. Nah, I can't do it, mate. It's me conscience, see.'

Owen nodded. 'That's very commendable, boyo. I fully understand. It's not often you come across a man with such a fine upstanding conception of his duty.'

'Yus, well. It's yer effics, innit?'

'Quite so, boyo. Quite so.'

'Well, I'll be off then.'

'Righto, boyo. Oh, just a minute. How's she going to get in? You'd better give me the keys to give to her. Otherwise she won't be able to get in, see.'

A grin crept furtive across the ethical lips of Frederick Fingers Hughes. 'Cor, yer a crafty one. But I got to deliver 'em, like the lady said.'

'Deliver them?'

'Number 2. Dahnstairs. She said to give' em to the geezer wot lives in number 2. Pacific, she was. The geezer in number 2 and no one else, she said. Quite pacific, she was.'

Owen Davies leaned on the first-floor banister and looked down at the door of the new tenant's room. 'The bastard,' he said.

Fingers Hughes sighed. 'Rival, is 'e? Maternal triangle, an' all. Seen it time an' again. Ruddy maternal triangle.'

'Get stuffed.' said Owen Davies, heading for his room.

'Yer what?'

'Get knotted,' suggested Owen, slamming his door behind him.   Fingers Hughes shook his head slowly and descended the stairs. 'Corst, 'e *is* Welsh,' he muttered to himself. 'E *is* foreign an' all, Gawd 'elp 'im.'

Lying on the floor inside Owen's door was a note from Georgia. It was brief and clear.

'Owen,' he read. 'I'm sorry, but I think we should break it off. We were never right for each other, I know that now. I'm sorry, but there it is. It was marvellous while it lasted and I'll always remember you. I hope we can still be friends. Georgia.'

Owen sat on his bed and read it through again. For God's sake, *friends*.

'Shit,' he said and remembered she hated him saying it. 'Shit,' he said again.

Jawaharlal MacGregor had not experienced much job-fulfilment during the day. He had spent most of it sweeping platforms, steps and endless tunnels of tiled underground corridor. Newspapers, sweet wrappings, pamphlets, cigarette packets and stubs, spent matches – there seemed no end to the debris people left behind. Occasionally he would discover a small coin and generally it was foreign. He had encountered items of underwear, an envelope containing nothing but hair, and a pair of false teeth. He felt he was in danger of developing a firm loathing for humanity in

95

bulk. Over the years he had become accustomed to the stale smell of the Underground – the sweat, the carbon dioxide, the fug of nicotine, the tired tang of warm metal. But he knew he would never completely accept the grime and the jetsam. Even worse was the bustle of clumsy feet and thrusting hands at the rush-hour barrier, his fingers grasping at tickets as the mass surged past, his brain blurred with calculating the fares, his eyes aching with watching for bilkers. And all day there had been the steady throbbing of his body busy breaking down Godfrey Thackeray's alcohol.

As he came away at the end of his shift Jawaharlal MacGregor thought of Kasturbhai and Emily. He thought of Simeon and Jagdish and Rajiv and Elizabeth and Indira. He thought of his 25-inch television set and the wet clothes hanging in the kitchen. He thought of all these things and at the end of Beckett Street he stepped from the pavement through the frosted doors and into the Excalibur bar of the King Arthur.

At one end of the counter sprawled Owen Davies. 'Mac!' he cried, draping an arm around Jawaharlal's shoulders. 'Speak up, bach. What's it you're having and God rot the rest of the world, all right.'

He ordered a pint and Jawaharlal sat on the neighbouring stool.

'Up your nose, boyo,' said Owen, swilling deep. 'Up your nose, you old sod, and we'll make this a night to remember, by God, isn't it?'

Jawaharlal giggled again, apologetically, 'Is wife. She is making all manner of goddam ructions when she is knowing I am drinking.'

'Stuff her, then. Begging your pardon,Mac, seeing as how she's your legal and that, but stuff the woman. Stuff 'em all, the whole bloody lot. Who the hell do they think they are?'

'Mine is thinking she is wife. She is also quite correct in that, goddammit.'

'To hell with her.' Owen waved his glass. 'Can't a man have a drink with his mates, look you? Sod 'em all, see?' They peered into their glasses. 'You having trouble at home, is it?'

'My God. Is like Tower of Babel. Is all speaking at once and goddam television loud all night. Is five children banging about flat like they all become carpenters and two women, two women making incessant demands.'

'Sure you have problems, boyo. One woman is one woman too many and that's for sure, God's truth.'

'Two women, goddammit, like vultures.'

'Believe me, it is my sympathy you have. It should not happen to a man, Mac, least of all a fine little man like you.'

'Is not so much big black one, you are understanding. Is little wife is worst. Goddammit, nag nag nag it is, like machine-gun at dawn.'

Owen leaned over and laid his hand on Jawaharlal's shoulder. 'Try thumping her, boyo. Bat the old bag one across the chops.'

Jawaharlal nodded slowly. 'This I am thinking. This I am considering seriously. I am not man of violence, you are understanding, but I am seriously considering physical sanctions.'

'That's it, boyo. Give her a good hiding, like. Anyway, to hell with them. Drink up, see. Drink up. Let's get them in again.'

Georgia knocked on his door. He was reading a paperback. 'Hullo, Patrick,' she said.

'Hullo.'

She was nervous. 'Did the locksmith leave my keys?'

He nodded at the table.'They're over there. In the brown envelope.'

'I hope you didn't mind.'

'Of course not.'

'I couldn't think of anything else.'

He said nothing. She picked up the keys. 'I'm having a little dinner party tonight.' she said. 'Will you come?'

He looked away. 'Georgia . . .'

'Please.'

'It's very sweet of you, Georgia, but . . .'

'Please, Patrick.'

'I've eaten already.'

'It won't be ready for a while yet.'

He shook his head. 'Thanks, but I'm awfully tired.'

She jangled the keys, fumbling with the envelope. 'I won't attack you, you know.'

'I didn't . . .'

'I'll behave myself.'

'I . . .'

'I promise. *Please* come.'

He hesitated, hating his weakness. 'All right,' he said. 'Thanks.'

She smiled. 'Oh, marvellous. Seven o'clock?'
'Okay.'
'Great. See you then.'
'Right.'
When she had gone he stared at the paperback, not seeing the words.

10

Georgia had bought two candles and they mounted flickering sentinel over his fears at either end of her small table. The fire spat red warmth into the room, hissing with warning.

He saw she had laid only two places. A party? She smiled and jiggled a pan over the gas ring in the corner. She poured him sherry and spoke of her childhood and home and parents, of her job, her hopes and fears, and he nodded and listened. She referred to Owen Davies and the fact that she had had her lock changed, and she mentioned the other tenants and how only that evening Errol Taylor had delivered a copy of Godfrey Thackeray's novel. They drank cheap Spanish wine and ate sausages and mushrooms and she discussed love and loneliness and he nodded and listened. She fed him tinned fruit salad and carefully poured a brandy from a miniature bottle and when they sat back to smoke cigarettes she asked why she felt she could tell him so much and he smiled and shook his head. She played a Sinatra L.P.

and served coffee. She described for him her life and philosophy and she poured more coffee. She asked him about himself and learned nothing, and she knew as a woman can that this was not the time to insist. She fed the gas meter a coin and asked him without success to make love to her.

Owen Davies and Jawaharlal MacGregor had lost track of the number of pints of best bitter they had consumed. Despite protests from the landlord Owen had from time to time entertained the customers with song. He had already rendered 'Men of Harlech' and 'The Green Green Grass of Home' and had had to be dissuaded from continuing with 'The Ball of Kirrie-muir'. Beer formed pools on the counter and his trousers. At his side, straddling a stool, Jawaharlal MacGregor observed that the floor appeared to be some distance away and wondered whether his feet would reach that far should he decide to stand.

Owen jabbed him with his beer glass. 'Wake up, you little black beggar.'

'Oh indeed, yes. Two pints.'

'You don't have it in you to resent being called a little black beggar, is it, Mac?'

'Indubitably no. I am not worrying in least.'

'That's good, boyo, because that's just what you are, see. A tiny black leprechaun.'

'I am being called worse things in my time. Oh yes, indeed.'

'No, I'm wrong, see. You're no little black beggar, Mac. It's a little *brown* leprechaun beggar you are, boyo, is it not, look you? Let's see the half-moons.'

'Begging pardon?'

'The half-moons, like. On the fingernails it is, to tell the truth. No half-moons and it's a touch of the tar-brush you have.'

Owen Davies carefully and closely inspected Jawaharlal MacGregor's fingernails and after long evaluation pronounced them acceptable. 'Half-moons you have, bach. It's a white man you are, Mac, no matter what pigment. Landlord! Another pint for my little white leprechaun here.'

The landlord, small and apprehensive, leaned confidentially on the bar. 'Don't you think you've had enough, Mr Davies?'

'Do I hell. Fill 'em up.'

The landlord rubbed his hands together. 'It's not you, of course, Mr Davies. No, not at all. It's your friend. The darkie. A bit too much, I'd say. Perhaps you ought to see him home.'

Owen focused on Jawaharlal. 'Hey, Mac. How are you feeling, Mac?'

'Bloody hell, goddammit.'

Owen poked a finger at the landlord. 'Hear that, landlord? Hear what my little pink uncle said? Bloody well, he said. Bloody well, like. Set 'em up.'

'I don't want no trouble, Mr Davies.'

'Trouble is what you'll be getting, see, unless two pints are forthcoming.'

'You know best, Mr Davies.'

'Of course I bloody know best.'

Jawaharlal frowned and examined his watch. Then he giggled.

'Discrimination,' bellowed Owen. 'That's what it is

and for sure. A racialist, that landlord, see. A bloody fascist. You're not all that brown, Mac, anyway. Don't let it get you down.'

'Oh my goodness, indeed no.'

'Full of racialists, this country. English pigs. There's nothing wrong with you, Mac, my old friend. Nothing that a good scrub wouldn't solve.'

'I am not complaining, Owen boyo, indeed no.'

'For sure you're not, and that's a fact. Ever hear the one about the Jamaicans in Bradford?'

'Please be telling.'

'Well, boyo, d'you know why they've closed in the gaps at the bottom of the public lavatories in Bradford? To stop the limbo dancers getting in for free.'

Jawaharlal giggled. 'Is very funny.'

Owen patted his shoulder. 'You're a good little man, Mac, and that's a fact. For a wog you have a great sense of humour, boyo. I think I shall make you an honorary Welshman. I hereby name you the Black Prince. Arise, Prince Monolulu. Heard the one about the Jamaican woman?'

'I am thinking no.'

'There's these three women in the supermarket, see. English, Irish and Jamaican. Talking about what they do with the kids while they're out shopping. "Ai just leave them at home with the au pair," says the English bird. "Sure and there's no problem at all at all," says the Irish. "Oi jest shove 'em in me basket." Then there's the Jamaican. "I get mine to wet their lips," she says, "and I just press 'em up against the window". '

Jawaharlal belched and giggled. 'Is very funny,

that,' he said. 'Goddammit, I must be remembering that one for Emily.'

Twenty minutes after closing time Owen Davies and Jawaharlal MacGregor stepped from the King Arthur public house and progressed with precision down Beckett Street towards number 57.

'You're a good little feller, Mac.'

'You are also meeting with approval, boyo, and that is for sure, goddammit.'

They paced purposefully along in careful step. 'Would you be up to doing a friend a favour, like?'

'Anything indeed, Owen boyo, my friend.'

'I have some business to discuss with that Kew feller on the ground floor. I would like a witness, see. Would you be considering coming in with me?'

'Is not too much to ask.'

'Good boy, Mac.'

'Then I am facing wife and beating hell out of her if necessary.'

'That's the spirit, boyo. Rough the old hag up a bit.'

'I am thinking we are understanding each other.'

'God bless you, bach, for a brown Welshman.'

Owen Davies did not bother to knock on the new tenant's door. He wanted to give them no warning, knowing what to expect, needing only to hurt them and himself and relishing the prospect of pain. The door was unlocked and he walked in, Jawaharlal MacGregor at his back. In an armchair by the fire the new tenant was sitting reading a paperback.

In his room on the other side of the hall Errol Taylor

stretched out on his bed perusing the latest issue of *Escort,* biting strips from his fingernails and dropping them carefully into his wastepaper basket.

On the top floor Godfrey Thackeray typed urgently, ignoring the aching of his arms. Across the landing Mrs Prendergast informed her husband that it was too late now for anyone to call and she might as well be going to bed. In the room below her Georgia Shuttleworth, affronted, scrubbed vigorously at the plates soaking in her basin. In the basement Kasturbhai MacGregor and Emily Jackson sat side by side, silently, watching television. Kasturbhai's jaw was firm and every few minutes she consulted the clock on the mantelpiece. Two fat tears slid slowly down Emily's cheeks.

11

Jawaharlal closed the door behind him and hiccuped. 'Where is she?' said Owen.

Kew rested his book in his lap. 'Hullo, Owen,' he said.

'Stuff that, see. Where is she?'

'What?'

'You know what I'm talking about, boyo. Don't come the innocent with me.'

Behind him Jawaharlal hiccuped again and giggled behind his hand. 'I am thinking I am worse for wear,' he opined. ' I am thinking I am better going now.'

'You stay where you are,' said Owen. 'Where's Georgia?'

'I expect she's upstairs in her room.'

Owen advanced towards him. 'You expect, do you, boyo? You bloody expect.'

'Come on, Owen. What's this all about?'

'You know damn well what it's all about.'

Jawaharlal hiccuped. 'Oh my goodness,' he said.

'Look, you'd better sit down. Both of you.'

'Sit down, is it? All cosy-wosy, is it? Not likely, boyo. We're not here for a chat.'

'What are you here for, then?'

'I've come to beat the daylights out of you.'

'Both of you?'

Owen clenched his fists and belched. 'Don't get smart with me, boyo. Mac's just here as a witness, see.'

'Indeed yes. Excuse me.'

'What do you need a witness for?'

'He's just a witness. I want a witness, see. I can have a bloody witness if I want one, can't I?'

'Of course.'

There was a long silence. Jawaharlal hiccuped and swore. Owen swayed and clenched his eyes, shaking his head. 'Are you going to get up or do I thump you sitting down?' he inquired.

'I'd rather you didn't thump me at all.'

Owen peered at him. 'Who do you think you are anyway, boyo?' he said. There was no reply. He wiped an arm across his brow. 'Who are you, then? Who the hell are you?'

'You know who I am.'

'I know sweet f.a., see. You come here all mysterious, telling nobody anything, never doing any work. What do you do? Where do you go all day, hey, boyo?'

Kew shrugged. 'That's my business.'

Owen shook his head energetically. 'Don't get smart with me, boyo. Don't come over the clever dick. It's my business too now, see. What with Georgia.'

'What about Georgia?'

'You know damn fine what about Georgia.'

'Indeed yes, goddammit. Excuse me.'

'You know *damn* fine what about Georgia. She's my bird, see. I'm going to marry her.'

Kew smiled. 'Congratulations. I'm very glad to hear it.'

Owen Davies approached him and lunged unsteadily with his fist. 'You cheeky, smooth bastard,' he said.

'Goddammit,' said Jawaharlal. 'Is violence. I am not understanding violence. I am man of peace, yes indeed.'

Kew stood up and backed away from Owen, who steadied himself against the back of the chair. 'Yellow creep. Tell us who you are, yellow creep, boyo. Tell us what you do all day apart from bedding other fellows' women.'

'You don't know what you're talking about. If you think I'm after Georgia you couldn't be more mistaken.'

'I see, boyo. It's her that's after you, is it? It's her that's not good enough for you, is it? You don't fancy her then, is that it? Kew by name and queue by nature, hey? Got them queuing up for you, have you? What's wrong with her, then?'

'Come on, Owen. You're talking nonsense. There's nothing between Georgia and me. You're imagining it all.'

Owen stepped pointedly in his direction.

'I think I am better going now,' said Jawaharlal. 'Goddam hiccups.'

108

'Imagining, is it now?'

'I am not wishing to be party to violence. I am having family obligations.'

'Imagining, is it? What do you do then, like, that you can be lying around all day to wait for her new keys? What does she want a new lock on her door for, then, boyo? Hey? You tell me that before I push your dirty nose through the back of your head.'

'I am having two wife and five children,' insisted Jawaharlal. 'I am having already all violence I can handle, and then some. Too true.'

Kew assessed Owen Davies and felt sorry for him. One punch in the beer and he would be down. His hair was ruffled, face red, eyes bleary, his suit rumpled and stained. It was pathetic that he was so fond of Georgia.

'If you really want to know, Owen, I'll tell you.'

'What are you on about now?'

'I'm a student.'

'What's that supposed to mean, boyo?'

'Or rather I was a student. I've left university.'

'Student then, is it? What sort of student is that, then? Student of the boudoir, is it? Is that it? Student of the flaming boudoir. What degree do they give you, hey, boyo? A B.Ed.?'

'Medicine.'

'Go on, boyo, liar.'

'I was studying medicine. I wanted to be a doctor.'

'Is remarkable,' said Jawaharlal. 'Is indubitably remarkable. Doctor is distinguished. Wife is arguing you are hippy dropout and is insisting rudenesses. Now I am telling her doctor and man of culture. Is making her very angry, oh yes indeed, goddammit.'

Owen Davies considered the new development. They stood and looked at each other. Jawaharlal hiccuped in the silence. 'Bloody hell,' he remarked.

'What's that got to do with it?' asked Owen eventually. 'Who gives a tuppenny toss what you do? Who asked you anyway, see?'

There was no reply. 'Doctor is most respectable,' said Jawaharlal thoughtfully. 'Undoubtedly is making her angry as hell.'

Owen rubbed his eyes and turned for the door. 'Sod you all,' he said. 'I'm going to bed.'

When Owen had left Jawaharlal pressed his hands together and gave a little bow. 'Am honoured, doctor,' he said.

Jawaharlal explored the steps to the basement and gripped the rail as he went down. Kasturbhai and Emily looked up as he came in.

'Is no need to be telling me,' he said. 'Is after eleven o'clock. Is late. I am now sleeping.'

'Not yet,' said Kasturbhai. 'You are now sitting down and discussing.'

Jawaharlal closed the door. 'Is nothing to discuss. Is after eleven o'clock. Is late. I am now sleeping. Is nothing more to say.'

Kasturbhai gave a narrow smile. 'There is a great deal to say,' she said grimly. 'A great deal to discuss. Emily is having another child.'

An hour later 57 Beckett Street was in darkness. Only the children and Owen Davies slept, Owen snoring richly in expensive oblivion. Mrs Prendergast

110

stared at the ceiling, remembering. Godfrey Thackeray stared at the ceiling, hoping. Errol Taylor stared at the ceiling investigating his courage and finding it deficient. Mr and Mrs Jawaharlal MacGregor lay side by side in silent communication. Emily Jackson twisted the sheet to her face and wiped her eyes. The new tenant clambered wearily out of bed to answer a knock at the door. 'Stick 'em up,' whispered Georgia. 'Stick 'em up and get back against the bed. This is a rape.'

12

Godfrey Thackeray described the words CHAPTER TWO at the top of the page and sat back to consult his Muse. She did not appear to be at the top of her form this morning. True, he had completed the first chapter and she had already provided him with a title, *For They Shall See God,* a quotation from Matthew 5:8 with apologies to Jesus of Nazareth. But Godfrey found himself dissatisfied with the results of his labours.

After only one chapter his heroine had already begun to exhibit a strong will of her own. Pure of heart and body though she was Godfrey was having trouble keeping her in line. A wayward girl, her optimistic parents had named her Chastity and she had been blessed as it happened with long blonde hair, long slim legs and small, firm pointed breasts that tilted upwards. From the picturesque village of her birth and childhood she had set out for London with a vocation to do good, her mission in life being to spread various sweetnesses and light. 'My mission in life,' she had told her Mummy on page two, 'is to spread sweetness and light.' 'Jolly good, darling,' her Mummy had replied and jolly good it indeed was. As Godfrey remarked on page three it was not often that members of the younger generation dedicated their lives to spreading sweetness and light.

Unfortunately Chastity was already demonstrating by page eight that her conception of showing good will to all men was not the same as Godfrey's. Before the situation slipped completely out of hand he had brought the first chapter to a swift conclusion. But he was not happy. He suspected that as soon as he embarked on Chapter Two young Chastity would simply toss her long blonde hair and ignore him, striding boldly off on her long tapering legs. God must have felt the same when he had to evict his tenants from the Garden of Eden.

'Blast the girl,' said Godfrey, and went to make himself a cup of tea.

The trouble with Chastity was that because of her hair, legs and other attributes she was bound to encounter some difficulty in retaining her purity of body and soul. Godfrey understood this and wondered whether to create her instead with warts on her face and hair on her legs. But he realized that this new Chastity would have little trouble remaining pure. The whole point of the story must surely be that she was highly desirable and yet unattainable. It was a heck of a problem.

Godfrey sipped his tea and brooded over his typewriter, rereading the first chapter. Then he gave a little whimper and tore it up.

An hour and several cups of tea later he resolved to abandon the arrogant Chastity and conjure up instead a girl called Faith. 'Chapter One,' he typed. This time he, Godfrey Makepeace Thackeray, would be the master. He would give Faith a faint moustache – not ugly enough to deter would-be suitors but just sufficient to keep her in her place.

'Faith Hope,' he typed, 'sat in front of her mirror combing her long blonde hair. . .'

Errol Taylor consulted a file of lending tickets at his counter in the Borough Library, seeking truth. He picked his nose thoughtfully and considered the problem of Georgia Shuttleworth and his libido.

On her return from work the previous evening he had delivered Godfrey Thackeray's novel as promised. She had seemed to be in a hurry. Spruce, neat, handsome, he had suggested casually that they might have dinner together. She had said she already had a date for that evening. He had referred to the following evening, or the evening after that, or in fact any evening. She had recalled that she was pretty booked up.

Errol slotted a ticket into the file. He did not consider himself to be touchy but he had kept a close watch on the front steps from his window and apart from the drunken arrival at about 11 o'clock of Davies and MacGregor there had been no traffic either to or from number 57 Beckett Street. Thinking coolly and logically, therefore, it seemed that Georgia Shuttleworth had been making excuses to avoid him.

114

Errol primped his spectacles up his nose and admitted that he had at first felt annoyed. He had, after all, gone to a great deal of trouble to make himself presentable. He had bathed, shaved, and broken into his bottle of Ruffian, the Rugged Lotion For Masculine Men. But he soon came to realize that he had in fact experienced a lucky escape. It was strange but he had previously completely overlooked the fact that Georgia Shuttleworth's legs were overweight. And the more he thought about her the more defects he discovered. She smoked. She talked too loudly. She had an annoying habit of brushing her hair out of her eyes. With these conclusions Errol had drifted gratefully off to sleep.

This morning his opinion of Georgia Shuttleworth was unchanged. From his window he had seen her running down the front steps, late, to catch her bus to work, her hair straggly, her eyes puffy, and he found himself extending his finding to women in general. As they came in and out of the library he noticed how imperfect they were — black rings or bags under the eyes, pale complexions, spots, hairy moles, squeaky voices, too much make-up, sagging breasts, massive haunches, knobbly knees, varicose veins, thick ankles. It was remarkable, he thought, how revolting they were. And suddenly it came to him. In a moment of revelation, as he stood behind his counter in the Borough Library, Errol Flynn Taylor realized that Destiny had greater plans for him. Let ordinary men dissipate their energies on women. He had better things to do than to waste his time pandering to his lust. Had History's great men bathed, shaved and dabbed themselves with Ruffian? They had not. They had cultivated their minds. Some, of course, had hired women to attend to their bodily needs but otherwise they had concentrated on their intellects. Like St Paul — now *there* was a man who really understood women — like St Paul on the road to Damascus Errol discovered in one blinding instant not only his destiny but also that he had long been within reach of his fulfilment.

Books.

Books surrounded him. Books on every conceivable subject. Books piled as high as the ceiling as as far as he could see. For Errol Taylor life arrayed itself in dazzling new raiment. He had discovered himself, his identity. He was an intellectual, high of brow and noble of mind.

He gazed longingly down the silent avenues of literature in the Borough Library, dry with an ancient thirst. With new energy he jabbed his spectacles back up his nose. He would start this very lunch hour. He would choose a massive volume, old and musty. Who was Georgia Shuttleworth? He would spend his evenings with Plato and John Stuart Mill, with Homer and Macaulay, with Chaucer and Trollope. In the quiet hours of the night he would plough his psyche and seed it with genius.

'Robbins?'

Errol stared at the woman. She was thin and tired with wispy hair, a plastic shopping bag and two children with liquid nostrils. 'Sorry?'

'Robbins. 'arold Robbins.'

He smiled kindly. 'Ah yes, madam. Over there. The

fiction shelves. Under R.'

'Ta.'

'That's quite all right, madam.'

He watched her go and scratched his armpit. Harold Robbins indeed.

Jawaharlal MacGregor sat quietly in his little cubicle by the ticket barrier trying not to excite his hangover. It had been a terrible shock. Emily pregnant again. Nine mouths to feed. The patter of twelve tiny feet drumming through the flat.

He had leaned weakly against the door. 'Is true?'

Emily had wiped her eyes and nodded.

'Bloody calamity.' He had weaved over to the armchair and collapsed.

Kasturbhai was in control, thin-lipped and wearing her triumph well. 'Calamity indeed,' she agreed. 'It is the final straw breaking the camel's back.'

'Straw? Camel?'

'Merely a saying. Proverb. You would not understand such matters, being uneducated.'

'Is damn stupid saying, then. We are having neither straw nor camel either.'

'You are ignorant.' She hitched her sari importantly about her. 'Anyway, this is not time for literary discussions. It is time for reckoning.'

Jawaharlal tried to focus on her. He felt the initiative was slipping away. 'Reckoning? What reckoning? Is nothing to reckon. Emily is having new baby. Only reckoning is you are now having to find job.'

Kasturbhai's eyes glinted. 'No more,' she said

firmly. 'I am sick and tired of this situation. I will not have further inconveniences. Emily will be leaving.'

Jawaharlal stared at her. Then he looked at Emily. She was crying quietly into her hankerchief. 'Leaving?'

'Leaving,' affirmed Kasturbhai. 'Going out the door with two children and big stomach and not coming back.' She sat stiff and upright, daring disagreement.

He struggled to assemble his mind. 'Is impossible,' he said finally. 'Is utterly impossible.'

Kasturbhai smiled dangerously. 'Impossible? How impossible? She is incapable of walking out the door? She is only five months pregnant. She is not yet on confinement bed. It is quite possible for her to walk out the door.'

Emily was dabbing her eyes. 'Look at her,' he said. 'You are reducing her to wreck. Are you having no feelings, woman? How is she working and feeding three children? You are telling me that.'

Kasturbhai smoothed her sari. 'This is no longer my problem. This is your problem and Emily's problem. I am washing both hands of further responsibilities. I refuse to tolerate further outrages.'

Jawaharlal smothered a belch. '*You* are not tolerating? *You* are not tolerating? Is I who is not tolerating. Not tolerating further insolence. I am master in house. I, Jawaharlal MacGregor. I am master and I am saying Emily is remaining.'

Kasturbhai shook her head. 'You are forgetting,' she said. 'You are forgetting original promises and conditions. You remember seven years ago? When I

118

have been arriving from Bombay?'

'I am remembering. I am also regretting.'

'It is too late for regretting. I am your wife. I am the mother of legal children. You possess responsibilities and obligations. It is useless regretting.'

Jawaharlal blinked and frowned, concentrating on her face. She was completely confident. 'When I have arrived from Bombay,' she said, 'I have found you with this woman. I, the legal wife, have found myself the outcast in my own husband's house. Nevertheless through much goodness of heart and considering the woman's advanced pregnacy I was allowing her to remain a few months. Do not interrupt. It is *I* who was allowing her to remain, not you. It is *I*. She is saying "you are a good woman, Kasturbhai" and she is correct. I was doing it from Christian charity. But what is this few months? Seven years. One more bastard child. Now third bastard child on the way. I will no longer allow immoralities under my own roof. Seven years ago you have promised it is only a temporary situation. Now time is up. She must go.'

Jawaharlal picked a strand of thread from the arm of his chair. 'Goddammit,' he said.

Emily blew her nose loudly. 'She is right, mister.'

'She is heartless monster.'

'No, no, Kasturbhai is a good woman. She is a good wife. She has made a lot of sacrifices. She has been very good to me. I am grateful. I can understand. I will leave tomorrow.'

'Leave? Where is it you are going?'

'I will find a place.'

'How are you living?'

119

'A woman has ways.'

'What is this?'

'I am not too old yet, praise the Lord.

Jawaharlal turned on his wife. 'Are you seeing what you are doing? Are you understanding full consequences of actions?'

'It is not consequences of my actions. It is not I am father of new child.'

'Goddammit, woman.'

Kasturbhai sniffed. 'It is not I am adulterer and blasphemer.'

'I am hoping for once there is God,' declared Jawaharlal with menace. 'I am hoping there is heaven and hell so you are being dispatched to correct place.'

'The Lord will judge,' said Kasturbhai, 'not you.'

'In this house is I will judge. I am judging Emily is staying.'

Kasturbhai stood up. 'I am not arguing. I am telling you she is leaving. I am giving you one week to find a new place for her.'

'And when I am refusing?'

Kasturbhai smiled. 'If you are so foolish to refuse I shall employ ways to make you keep your promise.'

'Ways? What ways?'

'Just ways. I am giving you one week and no more. Otherwise you are sorry. Goodnight, Emily. I know you are understanding.'

Emily nodded. 'You are a good woman, Kasturbhai. You have always been very kind.'

Kasturbhai nodded. 'Yes,' she admitted. 'Yes, that is true.' At the door she turned. 'I hope you find a better man in your new life. It is most highly unfortunate you have three children by ignorant drunkard.'

She went out and closed the door. Jawaharlal struggled to steady his nerves. He felt that this might be the moment to put his theories of marital violence into practice but he doubted his ability to stand up straight, let alone to wield his belt. Emily sat with her hands in her lap, fingers entwined.

'Is definitely true?'

'Yes. I saw the doctor today. Five months, he said.'

'Five months, goddammit.'

'I didn't notice before.'

'Is definitely mine?'

She began to cry again. 'How can you say that?'

'I was simply asking. Is wise to establish facts right.' He waited until she had dried her eyes. 'She is bluffing. She is playing politics. Tomorrow she is asking mink coat and saying no more about child.'

Emily shook her head. 'She is serious.'

Jawaharlal was belligerent. 'I too am serious. Goddammit, who is it wearing pants in this house? That I am wanting to know. You are staying.'

'We did promise. When she first arrived.'

'To hell with promise.'

'She is your wife.'

'You are proper wife. She is merely legal wife.'

'She has rights. I have none, mister. None.'

'You are number one woman. I am protecting you from this evil wife.'

Emily had begun to cry again.

Now, in his cubicle by the morning ticket barrier, Jawaharlal felt less confident. Was a verbal promise legally binding? Could she take him to court? And what were these 'ways' she had referred to? What could she do if he refused to budge? Life might become somewhat unpleasant but could she actually do anything?

'Goddammit, Emily,' he muttered. Why had she let it happen? She had been so careful since the last time. What had gone wrong? Of course, it happened all the time. India was peopled with accidents. Even in civilized Britain civilized knowledgeable couples suddently found themselves considering the prospect of nappies and disturbed nights. And to some extent Kasturbhai was right. They could not manage the burden of another child. God knew it was bad enough with five around the place, thumping about, yelling, whining, fouling the furniture. Another would make life hell. He could not afford it, either. They only just managed now on his and Emily's pay. Life would become intolerable.

They would have to get rid of it. That was the only way. Once Emily was no longer pregnant life would return to what it had been. It was only the child that had aroused Kasturbhai to give her ultimatum. Once that no longer threatened she would have to accept the situation and carry on as before. Jawaharlal nodded to himself. He was not sure how these things were accomplished but he knew they were possible. Perhaps Emily would know. If not they could seek medical advice. 'Oh my goodness,' he remembered. Through the haze of the previous evening he recalled Owen Davies and the new tenant. 'Who are you, boyo?' Owen had asked. 'What do you do, then?'

122

And he had replied: 'I'm a doctor.'

Jawaharlal MacGregor balled his fist. 'Goddammit, yes.' He did not fully understand why a doctor should be living in one room in number 57 Beckett Street, nor how his patients allowed him to lie around the place all day. But he suddenly saw an answer to his problem. Kasturbhai would never be able to resist the blandishments of a man of medicine.

Jawaharlal grinned and accepted a ticket from a passing traveller.

13

It was years since Georgia had felt so happy. Something within her was released, some deep exuberance that she had forgotten until Patrick reminded her. They said you always remembered your first lover, that even in death his lips materialized before your fading consciousness. She hoped it would not happen to her. Her memory of that particular milestone was of an urgent youth with acne called Norman who had sworn eternal passion in the back of his father's car and had left her fifteen seconds later feeling soiled and guilty. There had been a few since that first encounter but even with Owen she had felt no more than brief contentment. With Patrick it was different. She was excited, alive, prepared for miracles. She knew it was nothing physical — that had been nothing special. It was something more important. She felt as though she had won some victory over herself, that she had liberated herself from her past. With Patrick she was whole and her excitement was one of discovery. Who cared about emancipation and Women's Liberation and the desperate quest for orgasm? Her search was for more that nervous physical jerks. With Patrick she knew she could discover complete fulfilment.

As she climbed down from the top deck of the bus she was conscious of the conductor's eyes on her knees. The evening was already dark and wisps of mist hung soft among the trees. Behind her a man's heels clattered against the pavement, following her. She hurried towards 57 Beckett Street, turned gratefully in at the gate and shut the front door quickly behind her.

Later they lay close and warm.

'Mmmm,' she said. 'That was nice.'

Kew sighed. She smiled and touched his cheek. 'What is it?'

'Is anything inevitable?'

She explored his eyebrow. 'Yes.'

'I don't believe it.'

'Why?'

'It's indecent. It's an affront to human dignity.'

She laughed softly. 'We both knew.'

He was silent.

'We had no choice.'

He turned away, towards the wall, tucking his arm beneath his head. 'Keep away from me,' he said.

'What?'

'It's still not too late. You don't know me. Keep away.'

She laughed. 'Not a hope.'

He stared at the wall, attempting in the dark to decipher the pattern on the paper. He lay still. She was silent for a while, expecting explanations. A bus mut-

125

tered past in the road outside. A few minutes later the front door slammed and she could hear footsteps creaking heavily up the stairs. 'Tell me,' she said.

He said nothing.

'Tell me about it,' she said.

He stared at the wall for a while and them climbed out of bed.

'Like some coffee?' he said.

Owen Davies hesitated on the first-floor landing. He looked across at Georgia's door. The new lock twinkled at him. He had to try once more. He had felt there was something honest about Kew's denial that he was after her. Perhaps it had nothing to do with Kew. Perhaps it had all been his own fault. Owen realized that sometimes he had taken her a little for granted.

He knocked on her door and listened. There was no reply. She should be home by now. He switched off the landing light and stood by her door but the room was in darkness. Maybe it was not the new tenant at all. Maybe it was someone he knew nothing about, some smooth creep in the city. Maybe she was with him now, sitting with a married man in a West End restaurant, preparing with sherry for expensive sin inspired by prawn cocktail, coq-au-vin and Crêpes Suzette. Owen tried to imagine the man, balding, in his forties, his wallet as substantial as his gut.

He turned towards his door and heard her laugh drift faintly up from the floor below. Owen stood still and heard it again.

He barged into his room, snapping the light on and slamming the door, trembling. He swore without imagination for a full half-minute, calling down on Patrick Kew the curses of a dozen deities.

Ten minutes later, on his way out to the pub, he passed Jawaharlal MacGregor at the gate.

'Coming for a pint, Mac?'

Jawaharlal shook his head. 'I am having urgent business.'

'Come on, just a quick one.'

'No, no. Many thanks, but I am having no time.'

'She won't eat you, boyo.'

'Please?'

'Your wife. Did she play up last night?'

Jawaharlal rubbed his nose. 'Atmosphere was somewhat strained,' he said.

'To hell with her, bach. Show her who's boss, see. Did you thump her?'

Jawaharlal nodded energetically. 'I am asserting myself. Yes, indeed.'

'That's the spirit, boyo. But don't weaken. It's a great mistake to weaken, see. Come out for a couple of pints and if you get more trouble thump her again. It's all they understand.'

'Is quite true. I am in full agreement. You are man of wisdom. But not tonight since I am having business in hand.'

Owen shrugged. 'Suit yourself,' he said.

Further along the pavement he met Errol Taylor hurrying home with a pile of books. There's a dark horse, thought Owen. He looks as meek as anything and he turns up at her door in the middle of the night.

'Evening, boyo.'

Errol stopped and blinked. 'Good evening, Mr Davies. Are you out for your constitutional?'

Owen grinned. 'You might say that, bach. I'm off to the pub, like. Fancy a couple of pints?'

'Well, how kind . . .'

'Come on then, boyo. We're wasting good drinking time. They'll be closed in a few hours.'

Errol shook his head. 'It's very kind of you but I have a lot to do tonight.' He nodded down at the books. 'Political philosophy, you know.'

'Suit yourself, then. Only take it easy, see. You can get drunk on that sort of thing.'

In the Excalibur bar of the King Arthur he sat on a stool next to an old man in a mackintosh. 'Cheers, boyo,' said Owen, but the old man appeared to be deaf.

Jawaharlal let himself into the flat. The children roosted in a row on the sofa, dressed for bed, watching television. 'Hello, my children,' he said. 'I am home.'

A woman was brandishing a packet of detergent. 'Ma uses that,' said Simeon, 'but it doesn't work. It hasn't made her white.'

'It made *her* white,' said Jagdish, pointing at the screen. 'Look, Simeon. *She's* white. It worked for her.'

'It works for some people quicker. It's working for your Ma and you but not for my Ma and me. See? You're whiter.'

128

'Will we be all white one day? Like her?'

'Of course, stupid. Everyone gets white in the end. You have to be white when you go to heaven, like angels. That's why you have to keep having baths and washing.'

'I'm going to wash every day,' said Jagdish. 'Then I'll go to heaven before you.'

'Where is heaven?' asked Rajiv. 'Is near super-market?'

Jawaharlal muttered and wandered through to the kitchen. He felt uneasy. There was usually a good smell of cooking by the time he reached home and tonight there was nothing. Kasturbhai was sitting in a chair reading a newspaper. That was odd. Emily was drying some plates.

'I am back,' he said.

Emily smiled.

'This we know,' said Kasturbhai. 'Since you are standing here in the kitchen it is reasonably obvious you are back. There is no need to tell us.'

'I am always telling you.'

'This too we know. It is like a ritual.'

Jawaharlal pondered her and restrained himself. This was no time to arouse the woman. He glanced round the kitchen. 'What is happening?'

Kasturbhai looked up from the paper. 'Imports up again, exports down. Financial crisis. Balance of payments unhealthy.'

'What?'

'Also new trouble in Middle East.'

Jawaharlal inhaled deeply. 'I am not meaning that. I am meaning what is happening here, tonight, in

129

kitchen?'

'Emily is drying dishes. I am reading the newspaper. You are standing in the doorway.'

Jawaharlal counted slowly to himself. 'I am saying question differently. I am now asking why there is no cooking. I am asking what a man can be expecting to eat when he is returning exhausted after long day earning family necessaries.'

Kasturbhai folded her paper. 'You are hungry?'

'Is correct. I am hungry.'

'You wish for a meal?'

'If such wonders are possible.'

Kasturbhai stood up. 'Certainly. No problem. Baked beans.'

'Baked beans?'

'It would make a nice change. Also extremely nutritional, as seen on television.'

'We are never eating baked beans.'

'It is a nice change, then.'

'Goddammit!' Jawaharlal looked at Emily. She nodded quickly. 'Is true,' he said. 'Baked beans are making welcome change.'

He glanced through into the other room. On the screen a man was pointing a gun at another. 'Kill him,' said Simeon. 'Go on, kill him dead.'

They sat by the fire sipping coffee, Kew in his chair and Georgia squatting on the mat with her legs tucked under her. She looked up at him and felt comforted, warm and close. The sound of the television in the basement penetrated the room and accentuated its quiet. From above came the distant

130

spasmodic tattoo of Godfrey Thackeray's typewriter.

'Tell me.'

'What?'

'Everything. About yourself.'

He shifted in his chair. 'There's nothing important.'

'I don't care. I want to know.'

He sucked at his cup, warming his hands around its side. 'Why?'

'I'm interested. In you.'

'You know me as well as anyone.'

'That's not enough.'

He spread his legs towards the fire and she nestled closer, leaning back against his chair and resting her head in his lap. They sat together in silence and he began to stroke her hair. 'What do you want to know?'

Jawaharlal was surprised to find them together. At his knock she had moved away but he was embarrassed to discover that Owen had been right after all. 'I am sorry,' he said. 'Please be excusing intrusion.'

'That's all right,' said Kew. 'Come in.'

Jawaharlal closed the door and coughed into his hand. The girl smiled at him. 'Is good to be seeing you again, Miss Shuttleworth, oh yes indeed.'

'Coffee?' asked Kew.

'Oh yes, thank you, very good.' Perhaps she would go away when she had finished her coffee. Jawaharlal took note of the rumpled bed. No, perhaps she would not.

Kew produced a chair and sat him down.

'Did you enjoy the party?' she said.

'Oh yes, indeed.' He giggled. 'Mind you, is possible

131

I am perhaps overindulging taste for whisky.'

'Isn't that what parties are for?'

'Yes, yes.' What a splendid woman. 'Only I am hoping I am not behaving badly.'

'Of course not.'

'Sometimes I am behaving badly on account of whisky. These reports are occasionally reaching me later.'

She smiled again. They sat and looked at each other, expecting conversation. Kew urged coffee from the gas ring.

'You are enjoying party?' ventured Jawaharlal.

'Oh yes. It was great fun.'

'Yes, yes.'

'It's a good thing to get together now and then, don't you think? I mean, we'd never met before properly, had we?'

'Oh yes, indeed not.'

'It's stupid living on top of each other and never saying more than good morning, isn't it? I thought it was a marvellous idea of Mr Thackeray's.'

'Oh yes. Excellent idea. Is very good chap, Mr Thackeray. Is cultured too, I am told.'

'I'm reading his book.'

'Oh yes. I am believing it is excellent book.'

'I haven't actually started it yet.'

'Oh yes, yes.'

They smiled at each other and waited for Kew. The music from the television below welled up and squeezed through the floorboards. Jawaharlal started. 'Goddammit, is loud.'

She smiled.

'Is terrible loud,' he said, concerned. 'Dr. Patrick, why are you not mentioning volume on television? Is too loud for comfort in here.'

Kew carried the cup over. 'It doesn't bother me.'

'No, no. Is too much volume. Is damn kids. Five of them you are understanding, and two women. I am giving instructions to be turning it down. You are not possibly working in here with television of such quantity.'

'Honestly, it doesn't bother me. Really.'

'I am insisting. Is utter disgrace.' They sat and smiled at him. 'Is out of the question,' he said.

They drank their coffee, Jawaharlal eyeing the girl, willing her to go. She emptied the cup and sat back on the mat, wrapping her arms around her legs, prepared for a long siege. He burrowed into his coffee seeking a solution. Could he ask her to leave? No, that was impossible. It would be rude.

'Well, it's nice to see you again,' said Kew.

'Oh yes, very good. Is very pleasant to be drinking coffee.'

They both smiled at him. Jawaharlal knew he had to say something. 'Dr Patrick . . .'

Kew shook his head. 'I'm not a doctor, Mr MacGregor.'

Jawaharlal put his cup down. 'Yes, yes. You are saying only last night you are doctor. You are telling boyo Owen.'

'No, no. Medical student, I said, not doctor. Medical student.'

Jawaharlal nodded. 'Is right. Studying for doctor.'

'That's right. I was. Not any longer.'

Jawaharlal smiled with relief. 'Is very respectable, medical man. I must be remembering to be telling wife. She is being damn fed up.'

Georgia looked at Kew and raised an eyebrow.

'I am wishing advice,' said Jawaharlal. 'Advice of medical nature.' He inspected his feet. 'Is not matter I am wishing to discuss with my doctor. Is delicate affair, most personal.' He looked at Georgia. 'Is most personal indeed.'

'Do you want me to go?'

Jawaharlal waved an arm. 'Oh no, no. Indeed not.'

'Go on then,' said Kew.

Jawaharlal swallowed and fidgeted with his fingers. Goddammit, he should have said yes.

'I am asking promise of secrecy,' he said. 'And is better I am starting at beginning. I am having two wife, you are understanding. However is certain small problem since one is not married – big black one is not married, you are understanding. . .'

As Jawaharlal told his story Georgia listened, intrigued. She had always assumed that the Mac-Gregors must be Muslims and that he was quite entitled to four wives if he felt that way. Owen had joked about it. 'He obviously likes variety,' he had said. 'One black and one brown and he's still allowed two more. You'd better watch it, see, Mongoose. He'll be after you and a Chinese bird.'

When he had finished they examined the problem in silence.

'You are understanding urgency,' said Jawaharlal.

Kew shook his head. 'I'm sorry, I can't advise you. You should go and see your own doctor.'

Jawaharlal spread his hands. 'You are medical. I am telling all this and you are not helping me?'

'I'm sorry, I'm just not qualified.'

'But you are medical.'

'Look, you can get it done on the National Health these days.'

Georgia cut in sharply. 'Not when she's five months gone, you can't.'

'It's probably too late, anyway. Nobody would do it.'

'Too late?' said Jawaharlal. 'I am not understanding. Is nine months before is too late.'

Kew was patient. 'At five months the child is fully formed. Very few doctors would be prepared to perform an abortion that late. Very few good doctors, anyway. It's murder, you see, by that stage. The foetus has become human.'

Jawaharlal had lost all track of the discussion. 'You are not helping, then?'

'It's too late, Mr MacGregor,' Kew said gently. 'Three months ago I might have been able to help. Someone could have helped, anyway. But now it's too late.'

Jawaharlal cupped his head in his hands.

'There must be *something* we can do,' said Georgia. 'What about the old gin and bath trick?'

Jawaharlal looked up. 'Gin and bath?'

'Just an old wives' tale,' said Kew.

'What is this gin and bath?'

'You have to drink as much gin as you can and lie in a hot bath, as hot as you can make it,' said Georgia.

'It doesn't work,' snapped Kew. 'Not at five months, anyway. You might harm the child.'

'I am trying gin and bath.'

'I tell you, it doesn't work.'

'You are not understanding, Dr Patrick. Is desperate situation. I am trying anything.'

'You ought to go and see your doctor. Explain everything to him. He might be able to do something.'

Jawaharlal stood up. 'I am thanking you, Dr Patrick,' he said. 'You are keeping secret?'

'Of course. But look . . .'

'Is very good. I am sorry to be troubling you.'

With the last of his pay Jawaharlal bought a bottle of gin at the King Arthur's off-licence counter and hid it behind the dustbin outside the basement door. The children were in bed and Emily and Kasturbhai sat watching television. Jawaharlal slipped out to the bathroom and switched on the water heater.

'You are having a bath?' asked Kasturbhai.

Goddammit. How did the woman know everything?

'I am having bath,' he said. 'Are there objections to having baths? Am I perhaps to be asking permissions for baths?'

'It is simply surprise. There is a saying that cleanliness is next to Godliness which I now find difficult to believe.'

They spent a couple of hours in front of the television set before Kasturbhai announced her departure for bed. When she had gone he explained to

Emily the solution to their problem. She was apprehensive. 'Is doctor,' he stressed. 'Is respectable medical man.'

At eleven o'clock they crept into the bathroom and she sank herself deep in the water. Jawaharlal officiated from a chair, feeding her gin and topping up the water every few minutes until she gleamed with heat.

By 11.15 he felt in need of a drink himself. By 11.45 Emily was giggling softly. Jawaharlal waved his arms. 'Perhaps I am getting in bath as well,' he said. 'Goddammit, maybe is needing father to be taking treatment too.'

By midnight Jawaharlal MacGregor and Emily Jackson were wedged together, head to feet and feet to head, in the bath in the basement of number 57 Beckett Street. Water slopped over the top onto the floor. Emily lay back with her eyes shut, giggling, her huge black body heaving the water into whirlpools. Jawaharlal began to sing.

The door opened and Kasturbhai stood and inspected them. Jawaharlal waved the gin bottle, his head jammed to the wall by a tap. 'Is wife, goddammit,' he yelled. 'See, wife, you are now understanding cleanliness is next to Godliness. Is plenty room in bath for three. Be getting in, woman, goddammit.'

He woke the next morning to find himself on the sofa in the living room. Emily was shaking his shoulder. 'Hey, mister,' she said. 'Kasturbhai. Kasturbhai has gone.'

14

Godfrey Thackeray contemplated with approval the matter of Faith Hope, her long blonde hair and her faint moustache. He always trusted his critical faculties first thing in the morning and as they reviewed Chapter One they provided congratulations. He had succeeded in making Faith desirable yet submissive to his will. Whenever she appreciated herself in the mirror, admiring the length of her hair, the firm upward direction of her breasts and the long, slim properties of her legs Godfrey had successfully moved her to notice also the dusty line of hair on her upper lip. She was, he decided happily, a girl who would go far, certainly the requisite 60,000 words.

He had brought her in Chapter One from the quiet and picturesque country village of her birth to the seething vitality of the city. 'Mummy,' she had remarked on page two, 'my mission in life is to spread sweetness and light. 'Jolly good, darling,' her Mummy had replied and jolly good it indeed was. As Godfrey pointed out on page three it was not often that members of the younger generation dedicated their lives to spreading sweetness and light. He was not yet sure what form this selflessness would take but he had rented for her a room on the first floor of an old suburban house, peopling the rest of the house with a family of immigrants, three assorted young men and, on the top floor, a retired lady and a middle-aged painter of unrecognized genius. One of the young men, a Welshman living on the same floor as Faith, had helped her carry her suitcases up from the taxi when she arrived. Godfrey made a note in his diary to discover what the women's magazines paid for serialization rights.

He heard a clank from the front gate and looked down from his window to see the postman's bicycle propped against the pavement wall. Godfrey gathered his dressing-gown cord around him and walked jauntily down to accost the morning mail. There was never much for him, apart from the literary magazines and an occasional abusive anonymous letter from his dear dead wife's relatives, but Godfrey knew that it often took the film companies several months to get round to making their offers. One of these days an urgent contract might arrive offering thousands for *His Own Sweet Will* and it would be unseemly for the envelope to lie on the hallstand for days hoarding dust.

He paused on the first-floor landing to see Georgia Shuttleworth emerging from the new tenant's room down below. Odd. Godfrey looked at his watch. Not yet eight o'clock. He smoothed his hair.

She came up the stairs in a hurry, dressed in a man's raincoat and carrying her clothes in one hand.

Her feet were bare and her hair tousled. He was surprised to discover that without her make-up she carried on her upper lip a faint trace of hair.

'Mr Thackeray!'

He bowed his head. 'Miss Shuttleworth. Good morning.'

She clasped her clothes in both hands, rolling them tightly together. 'I heard the postman,' she said.

'Indeed. And I too. Is there anything for me?'

She glanced down the stairs. Two letters and a wrapped magazine lay on the mat. 'A magazine,' she said. 'Yes, there's a magazine.'

'Excellent.'

She flicked hair from her face. 'I must dash or I'll be late for work.'

He stood aside. 'Of course.'

In the hall he collected the magazine and tapped it against his lips, contemplating the new tenant's door. He frowned, considering the implications for Faith Hope and her calling. He climbed the stairs slowly.

Back in his room he primed the kettle and scattered cornflakes in a bowl. There was obviously more to Faith Hope than he had expected. While she appeared to encourage the Welshman who had helped her up the stairs with her suitcases she was secretly involved with another inhabitant of the house, the surly, rude young stranger who lived on the ground floor.

As the kettle bristled towards its climax Godfrey scanned his face in the mirror, mowing it with his electric razor. What could they have in common, the demure but desirable country girl and the sullen, mysterious young man? What was going on? Who was this person, anyway?

The kettle wailed. Godfrey put it out of its misery. He prepared the radio for the news and sat at his desk with the cornflakes. He rejected the obvious solution. Faith was not like that, she was not that sort of girl. So why had she been creeping from the young man's room carry a ball of clothing early in the morning?

From the radio the announcer mentioned the Laotian peace proposals and an American race riot. Godfrey chewed steadily through his cornflakes, carefully blotting the milk from the corners of his mouth. Why should a girl like Faith do a thing like that? What was the new tenant's hold over her?

The announcer paused momentarily and broadcast the shuffle of a turning sheet of paper. Then his voice beamed clear across the airwaves. 'The body of a young woman was washed up late last night on the beach at Eastbourne. Police have issued the description of a man they believe may be able to help them with their inquiries. He is Charles John Lowry, aged twenty-six, about six feet tall, slimly built, with dark hair and high cheekbones. He was last seen leaving his lodgings in Bournemouth three weeks ago. It is believed he may now be living in London.'

Godfrey stared at the radio.

'And now the weather. The forecasters say it will be a dry day over much of the country with temperatures . . .'

Godfrey put his spoon down. Three weeks ago? Twenty-six? Now living in London?

'. . . It will be dull over most of England and Wales

141

although . . .'

Six feet? Slim? Dark hair? High cheekbones?

'. . . occasional scattered showers. And now here again are the main points of the news. In Washington a White House . . .'

Godfrey half stood, half leaned against his desk. 'Dear God,' he said.

For a few minutes he sat on his bed, sharpening his teeth on his knuckles. Then he dressed quickly and stepped out of the house. A hundred yards down the road he looked quickly over his shoulder and opened the door of the telephone kiosk. Closing it carefully behind him he lifted the receiver and dialled 999.

Mrs Prendergast watched from her second-floor window as her clock clacked loudly on the shelf and Godfrey Thackeray hurried down the road. That was unusual. Mr Thackeray rarely left the house in the morning. The MacGregors came and went at odd hours and only half an hour earlier Mrs Prendergast had noticed the Indian woman and three children staggering along the pavement in the grey morning light carrying bundles. But apart from the new tenant the others all had fixed times of departure. The girl, the Welshman and the earnest young librarian tended to leave the house within minutes of each other, at a walk soon after eight o'clock, at a run towards 8.30. But Mr Thackeray never appeared until one o'clock, when he would walk briskly away towards the common, always returning at about three.

It was certainly odd. It was even odder that he should now be returning only a minute later. Mrs

Prendergast watched from the safety of her curtain as he turned in at the gate, glancing nervously at the new tenant's window. He came swiftly up the stairs, mounting them two at a time, and she heard him turn the key in his lock behind him. That too was unusual. He normally left his door unlocked. Mrs Prendergast frowned and sighed. Life became increasingly complicated. How could you rely on anything if people suddenly started leaving the house at odd hours and unexpectedly locking their doors behind them? People were so undependable these days. The old standards were disappearing. Even the pound had apparently been devalued again and was now worth no more than 100 pence. People were rude in the shops and she would not be surprised if the young woman in the Post Office was on drugs. It was all drugs and sex and rudeness nowadays. Mrs Prendergast blamed a great deal of it onto Harold Wilson. Things had not been the same since that nice Sir Alec was cheated out of being Prime Minister.

'You're lucky to be out of it all, Henry,' she nodded. 'Very lucky indeed. You're a lucky boy.'

Mrs Prendergast set out to discover her reading glasses. When they were safely on her nose she sat at the table and fondled her Bible. She wondered to which page she would be directed this morning. She always selected a single random verse as a text for the day, but for the past few mornings the Good Book had disappointed her, falling open at passages that appeared to have no possible relevance to her life. Yesterday it had been Genesis Chapter 5 and Mrs Prendergast had found it singularly unrewarding. The lifespans and reproductive habits of Seth, Enos, Cainan and their ilk did not strike Mrs Prendergast as being matters of great moment. Apart from experiencing a brief sympathy for Methuselah's father, Enoch, whose little life had been cut unreasonably short after 365 years, Mrs Prendergast had not reacted favourably to Genesis Chapter 5. Was there perhaps some significance for her in the fact that Noah begat no one until he was five hundred years old? Perhaps Henry had been responsible for her opening the Book at that page. Perhaps that was Henry's idea of a little joke. During his lifetime Henry had not been noted for his sense of humour but she could believe that had he now developed one it would exhibit a sepulchral quality. Henry could, of course, be extremely aggravating.

She held the book firmly, spine down on the table, and opened it decisively at Ezekiel Chapter 12. 'The word of the Lord also came unto me, saying, Son of man, thou dwellest in the midst of a rebellious house, which have eyes to see, and see not; they have ears to hear, and hear not: for they are a rebellious house.'

Mrs Prendergast closed the book slowly and replaced it on the table. She gazed out across the spindly branches of the autumn trees. 'He will come, Henry,' she said. 'It is surely written.'

From its vantage point in the window across the road the parrot swayed on its perch and nodded. Mrs Prendergast did not observe this phenomenon. She was remembering instead a gipsy fortune-teller and her reference to a tall, dark stranger whose appearance would transform her life.

Errol Taylor arrived early, a moment after the head librarian. 'Good morning, Mr Potter,' he said. 'I wonder if I might have a brief word with you?'

Mr Potter raised his eyebrows and regarded Errol Taylor over the top of his spectacles. Mr Potter was not a man of many words. A raised eyebrow and a lowering of spectacles were Mr Potter's invitation to speak.

'It's Plato,' said Errol. 'His historicism and his Law of Change.'

The head librarian examined Errol's eyes. Errol took this as a sign of encouragement. 'His Theory of Forms,' he elaborated. 'I am bothered by his methodological essentialism. We today, by contrast, tend to be methodological nominalists, and I wondered whether you would agree that we are wholly wise to be so. Don't you feel that there is something intrinsically attractive in his conception of the perfect prototype?'

Mr Potter lifted his nose and considered Errol through the lenses of his glasses. 'Mr Taylor,' he said. 'I haven't the faintest idea what you're talking about.'

Jawaharlal MacGregor stood on the platform and when no one was looking swung his broom over his head and gave a little skip of pleasure.

Life, he decided, was a marvel — a rich, hilarious paper chase furnished with banana skins. Even when everything was going well you could encounter a nasty surprise — but, equally, when the paper lay thin on the ground it could be someone else's turn to tread on peel and the sight was glorious to behold.

'Oh my goodness,' he giggled, shaking his head.

Kasturbhai was gone, Kasturbhai and those snivelling children of hers. Thin-lipped Kasturbhai, the scourge of Bombay, had taken her possessions and vanished, leaving him with soft, warm, smiling Emily burgeoning big and black and beautiful in her pregnancy. With one decision Kasturbhai had transformed him. He was once again in control. He was glad now that the treatment of gin and bath had been in vain. What was one more child now? Only three. A good number, three. Three smiling faces reflecting Emily. There was no need to trouble the doctor again. His prescription of gin and hot water had solved Jawaharlal's problem better than anyone could have imagined. What a stroke of brilliance it had been to step into the bath with Emily, what luck to be inspired to sing at midnight. He did not care where Kasturbhai had gone. Let her divorce him, let her do her worst. She had gone and that was all that mattered. 'And what about money, mister?' Emily had said. 'She is your wife.' And what about money? Let her have it. Three, four pounds a week. Jawaharlal swept vigorously. It was worth it. Well worth it. Goddammit, it was cheap.

Tonight they would celebrate, just he and Emily. The children in bed, just two children in bed, and he and Emily alone and free before the 25-inch television set. He would borrow some money from Chandra and buy a bottle of wine and he and Emily would engage in fervent passion in the kitchen. In Kasturbhai's kitchen, in tight-faced Kasturbhai's holy shrine, they would concoct such a recipe as would

146

widen her narrow eyes.

On his way home Jawaharlal bought a bottle of wine and danced briefly on the pavement as he approached 57 Beckett Street.

Emily was sitting crying on the sofa. The room looked strangely bare.

'Emily,' said Jawaharlal. 'What is matter? What is happening? Where is television?'

She ran heavily over to him and wept on his shoulder. 'They've taken everything.'

'What is this everything?'

'Everything except the landlord's things. The television, everything.'

Jawaharlal leaped through the flat, investigating. 'Goddammit,' he shouted. 'Even television! Is rented. Is not even paid for. Who is doing this? Goddammit, is monster Kasturbhai.'

'They came when we were all out. And there was something else. It was horrible . . .'

'Else? Horrible? What is this?'

'The bathroom. They . . .'

'Bathroom?'

'They . . . smeared things.'

'Smeared? What is these things?'

'Horrible . . . disgusting things.'

'What things?'

'Revolting things. In the bath, Jawaharlal. It was disgusting. All over the bath. I was nearly sick.'

Jawaharlal erupted. 'Goddammit, is monster wife. Is her family.' Then, a few mintes later, when Emily had dried her eyes: 'Is no matter. Is over now. She is welcome to furniture. She is welcome to be having

147

anything. So long as she is leaving us now in peace she can be having anything she is wanting.'

They celebrated with the wine and rested close together staring at the blank corner that had once been inhabited by a 25-inch television set. 'Is no matter,' said Jawaharlal. 'Is we together is all that is mattering,' and Emily smiled.

It was then that the first brick smashed through the bedroom window.

15

Godfrey Thackeray had always considered himself to be a good citizen, an upright man with a solid understanding of his civic obligations. He never dropped litter in the streets and had always attempted to pay his bills on the first demand. He had never travelled on a train without parting with the full fare and each Christmas he contributed to at least one charity, in rotation. As evidence of his social responsibility had not his first reaction on discovering the identity of the new tenant been to inform the police? Godfrey consulted his reflection in the kettle and nodded in agreement. Yes, that had undoubtedly been his first reaction. But just as he had finished dialling 999 he had on impulse quickly replaced the receiver.

Ever since the morning his wife had unaccountably failed to awake Godfrey had noticed himself acting impulsively. It was, he decided, the long-subdued artistic side of his nature at last asserting itself. He was coming to trust his creative instincts. Why had he suddenly replaced the receiver? Partly from doubt, perhaps. One did not wish to be over-hasty, did one? One had no real desire to make a fool of oneself. But Godfrey knew that that had not been the whole reason. 'Not at all,' he said, shaking his head at his reflection in the kettle. The real inspiration had been his Muse jogging his elbow and urging him not to be foolish. No doubt the shades of Shakespeare and Dickens had also squeezed themselves into the telephone kiosk. There had in fact been quite a literary party in the phone box at the end of Beckett Street and its outcome had been an agreement from all concerned that Godfrey's duty to Art transcended his social obligations. How many writers, Shakespeare had demanded, had been fortunate enough to be able to observe at close quarters a wanted killer on the run? Even Truman Capote had only examined his material after the police. Here was a remarkable opportunity to fashion Art from life. Was he, Godfrey Makepeace Thackeray, to sacrifice his genius to his social conscience? Was he the man to bury his talents beneath a wad of signed statements and skeins of red tape? Could he really sell his birthright for the gratitude of a chief constable? Of course not. 'Of course not,' Godfrey assured his elongated reflection. 'Unthinkable.'

He had tuned in to the news several times during the day and nothing he had heard had persuaded him to change his mind. True, one could understand the urgent desire of the Criminal Investigation Department to interview twenty-six-year-old Charles John Lowry. They had a female corpse in their possession

150

and the constabulary is notoriously offended by corpses whatever their gender. But, as Godfrey inquired of the kettle, would a couple of days' delay be so important? Just a couple of days, that was all he needed. Just two days to investigate the relationship between Charles John Lowry, alias the new tenant, and Georgia Shuttleworth, alias Faith Hope. Then, his duty to Literature accomplished, he would happily dispatch his duty to society.

Godfrey nodded and rewarded the kettle with water, plugging it into its socket. He had bought an evening paper and he examined again the front page. It displayed a photograph of a man the police believed could assist them in their search for the Beast of Eastbourne. Godfrey admitted to himself that it did not look exactly like the new tenant. The hair was a different syle, the nose a little too long, the jaw slightly square. But the photograph was fuzzy and the face was gaunt and the eyes demonstrated the same shiftiness he had recognized in the new tenant. Godfrey understood now the man's furtiveness. It all fitted in.

It was then that he heard a smashing of glass, as though a brick had been hurled through a window downstairs.

Georgia lay on her side, her head bracketed on the pillow by her arm. 'Mmm,' she said. 'That was nice.'

He smiled. She sighed, relieved. Ever since she had told little Mr MacGregor the night before about the gin and hot bath Patrick had been withdrawn. She tapped the tip of his nose with her finger.

'That's better,' she said.

'What?'

'Smiling. You were angry, weren't you?'

'No.'

'Yes you were. You were angry with me for telling Mr MacGregor.'

He lifted a strand of her hair and judged it against the light, letting it fall back across her face. She flirted with her eyes and he rememberd another girl and the way she too had looked at him that last night together. He turned away and closed his eyes. Would he never forget?

She touched him. 'What's the matter?'

'Nothing.'

'Come on.'

'It's nothing.'

'Tell me. Please.'

He shook his head. 'I'm just tired.'

'Of me?'

He hesitated. It had to stop, he knew that. He had to put an end to it. 'Of course not. I'm just tired.'

'Do you want to sleep?'

Yes, to sleep — and forget. 'I won't be able to sleep.'

'Do you want me to go?'

He appraised her — so reasonable, so eager to please, so vulnerable. Yes, go, go. Leave me alone. 'No,' he said.

She wrapped him warm with her arms and pressed his head into her shoulder. He closed his eyes and felt her body with his hands.

'Patrick,' she said. 'What do you do?'

'Mmmm?'

'What do you do? All day. Are you really a medical student?'

'I was.'

'Was?'

'I'm not any more.'

She eased herself closer, twining a leg over his. 'What happened?'

He burrowed his nose into her neck. 'I left.'

'Left?'

'Yes.'

'Just like that?'

'Yes.'

She looked over his head at the wall, not daring to move, to disturb the mood. 'So what now?'

He sighed. 'Nothing.'

'Nothing?'

'No.'

She frowned at the wall and stroked his back, her fingers urging him gently to dismantle the barrier that grieved her.

It was then that they heard the sound of breaking glass.

Across the hall Errol Taylor started in his chair and looked up from his book. The first crash was followed by a second.

On the top floor Mrs Prendergast crossed herself hurriedly and peered from her window. Two dark figures were racing away along the pavement. '. . . thou dwellest in the midst of a rebellious house,

153

which have eyes to see, and see not; they have ears to hear, and hear not: for they are a rebellious house.' Mrs Prendergast sat back in her chair and nodded. '*I* have eyes, Henry,' she said. 'I have both eyes and ears, and all in excellent condition.'

Owen Davies heard neither the first crash nor the second for the excellent reason that he was several miles away, leaning on the bar in the Plough and Gosling and considering the manner in which the barmaid's legs encountered each other just above the knee.

Jawaharlal MacGregor bounced to the door and up the steps to the front gate. He hesitated, panting. There were two of them. Jawaharlal had never overestimated his courage. Their heels clattered away from him along the pavement. They passed briefly through a distant slab of lamplight and vanished, the patter of their shoes leaking faintly away into the darkness.

He turned to see Emily standing in the bright doorway to the basement, her fist at her mouth. The main door to the house opened and Godfrey Thackeray advanced towards him.

'I heard glass,' said Godfrey. 'Breaking glass.'

Jawaharlal nodded vehemently. 'Is goddam hooligans.'

'Hooligans?'

'Indeed, sir. Look, my windows. Is smashing two window with bricks, goddamit.'

Godfrey examined the evidence from the outside. 'Good Lord. Hooligans, you say? You ought to ring

154

for the police.'

'No,' said Emily. 'Jawaharlal, please. Not the police.'

Godfrey noticed the new tenant had appeared at the door. Good Lord, no, not the police. Not yet, anyway. 'No,' said Godfrey. 'No, perhaps you're right, Mrs MacGregor. They can be an infernal nuisance, the police.'

'The police?' said Kew. Georgia Shuttleworth materialized behind him. Godfrey summoned up all his faculties. He would need to be alert.

'Hooligans, Dr Patrick,' said Jawaharlal. Godfrey frowned. 'Goddam hooligans breaking windows.'

'We ought to discuss this,' said Godfrey. 'This vandalism affects us all. Perhaps we could go inside?'

'I don't think . . .' said Kew.

'No, no,' urged Emily. 'Please. It is no trouble. I could do with some company.'

Errol Taylor had joined the throng at the door. He jabbed a finger at his spectacles. 'What's up? What's going on?'

Jawaharlal waved his arms. 'Is hooligans,' he announced. 'Is goddam hooligans throwing bricks through windows. Two window, goddammit.'

'We must have a meeting,' insisted Godfrey. 'We must discuss this problem. It affects us all.'

'Come in, come in,' said Emily.

They followed her into the flat and squeezed into the available furniture. A brick lay on the floor, a piece of paper trapped to it by a rubber band. Jawaharlal picked it up. Four words were scrawled across it. 'Drunkard blasphemer adulterer filth,' it

155

said. He screwed it up and rammed it into his pocket.

'Evidence?' asked Godfrey.

'Is nothing. Just wrapping.'

Emily disappeared to reassure the children and assemble tea and biscuits. They sat uncomfortably close and discussed action. Godfrey mentioned the possibility of summoning the law and eyed the new tenant as he did so. He said nothing. Oh, cool, thought Godfrey. Very cool, Mr Charles John Lowry.

When Emily reappeared with a tray Jawaharlal was doing his best to dissuade them from involving the police. He had no wish to confront detectives. Soon after his arrival in Britain Chandra had been stopped on the street by a squad car and warned for walking at night without displaying lights both front and rear. One officer had pointed out that pedestrians would not be able to see Chandra coming the other way on a dark night. Even apart from such things Jawaharlal realized that questions would be asked and that they might be questions he did not wish to answer.

The conversation faltered as Emily distributed refreshments. Georgia inquired after Kasturbhai and learned that she had gone to stay with relatives.

'You really shouldn't have gone to all this trouble.'

'Oh, it's no trouble at all, Dr Patrick,' said Emily. 'No trouble at all. To tell you the truth, I feel in need of company after this evening.'

Godfrey leaned forward. 'I didn't realize you were a doctor.'

The new tenant looked down into his cup. 'Well, I'm not. There's been a misunderstanding.'

'A misunderstanding?'

156

'I used to be a medical student. Mr MacGregor . . .'

'Ah, a medical student.'

'Yes.'

'How fascinating.' Godfrey nodded and smiled encouragingly. 'That's very interesting. Tell me, as a medical man I'd value your opinion of this murder case.' He stared at him. 'This body they found on the beach at Eastbourne.'

'I'm sorry. What body is this?'

'It's all in the papers, radio, television. This young woman was washed up on the beach. The police are looking for a young man from Bournemouth, a Charles John Lowry.'

Godfrey paused, watchful. Lowry was cool, all right. 'I'm sorry,' he said. 'I don't read the papers much.'

'They say he could be on the run somewhere in London.'

'Yes?'

'This Charles John Lowry.'

'Oh.'

Errol scratched his nose and stirred his tea. He wondered how he had found himself involved in this tiresome gathering. Another couple of minutes and he could escape back to Plato. He would have to learn to ignore such distractions. He glanced across at Georgia Shuttleworth and noticed the rings under her eyes and the girth of her knees. That had been a narrow shave. Just as he had learned to reject the blandishments of women he would have to teach himself to resist the temptation to investigate broken windows in the night.

'What was it?' said the new tenant.

Godfrey frowned. 'I beg your pardon?'

'You were going to ask me something.'

'Was I? Oh yes, of course. How stupid. The body. Well, this young woman seems to have been in the sea for some time before she was washed ashore. I was interested — as a writer, you know, purely profession-ally — I was interested to discover how long she might have been in the sea.' There was no sign from Lowry that he was flustered. Godfrey found himself almost admiring him.

The new tenant emptied his cup. 'It would depend on the state of the body.'

'Ah.'

'You'd have to ask a forensic expert who had examined it.'

'Yes, of course.'

'Is this for a new book?' asked Georgia.

'Well, yes. I was only toying with the idea, you know.'

'How exciting. Is this how authors get ideas? From the news?'

Godfrey smiled modestly. 'Inspiration moves in mysterious ways,' he said.

'How fascinating.'

In the silence Errol Taylor slurped the dregs of his tea and rattled his cup. 'Well, I must be going,' he said.

'Me too,' said the new tenant, rising. 'Thank you so much for the tea.'

'No, please,' said Emily. 'Don't go yet.'

'I really must.'

158

'So must I,' said Errol.

Georgia conferred with her watch. 'I really ought to be off as well. I must write some letters tonight.'

They all left together, Godfrey lingering at the basement door discussing the possibility of forming a vigilante committee. 'Well,' said Errol as they reached the hall. 'Back to Plato.'

'Plato?'

'The Greek philosopher, Mr Kew. Famous thinker, you know. Lived about the fourth century B.C. I'm reading his works at the moment.'

'The *Dialogues* or the *Republic*?'

Errol frowned. 'You know them?'

Kew shrugged. 'I've read a bit.'

'Well, it's the *Republic,* actually. Well, well. Tell me, Mr Kew, I'm intrigued by his Theory of Forms, the idea of the perfect prototype. Would you say it was a valid ideal. Did it ever exist?'

Georgia panned to Kew and widened her eyes. He shook his head. 'Poor old Plato. Just another misguided idealist. Things don't change much either for the better or the worse. Everything is the same, always, for ever the same.'

Errol fidgeted excitedly with his glasses. 'But the philosopher king! What a magnificent conception, idealistic or not.'

'A blueprint for universal slavery, for totalitarianism. Even Plato came to accept the impracticability of his system. Did you know he tried it out in Sicily under Dionysius II of Syracuse? It ended in intrigue and bloodshed.'

'Did it?'

'Plato realized he was dreaming dreams. When you're through with the *Republic* try the *Laws*. There he sets his sights lower and comes up with a much more practical blueprint.'

'He does?'

'Yes. In fact Aristotle's *Politics* is extraodinarily similar to Plato's *Laws*. You might almost say the one was cribbed from the other, though to read Aristotle's attacks on Plato you'd think the old boy had never written anything other than the *Republic*. Not a very grateful pupil, was our Aristotle.'

Errol grinned weakly. 'Well, I'd better get on with it,' he said.

Back in his room he settled down with his book but the words sat close on the page and sharp and hostile. After a while he decided that Plato was perhaps best studied early in the morning. He closed the book and sought out another.

Behind the door opposite Georgia poked a finger into Kew's ribs. 'My God,' she said, 'and I thought you were just a pretty face.'

On the basement doorstep Godfrey made his farewells. 'I'm sorry not to have seen Mrs — er, the other Mrs MacGregor. Where is she staying?'

Jawaharlal looked swiftly over his shoulder. Emily was in the kitchen. 'I am not knowing,' he said conspiratorially. 'She is disappeared.'

Godfrey stepped back. 'Disappeared?'

'Disappeared, sir. Off face of earth. Poof. One minute is here, next minute gone. Between you and me is good riddance and Rest In Peace.'

Godfrey climbed the stairs swiftly, his mind in a

state of consternation. Safe in his room he locked the door and wondered whether he ought to install a couple of bolts as well. For a while, sitting on his bed, he weakened. As an honest citizen his duty was clear — he should call the police. The weakness passed. Far into the hours of the night the prattle of his typewriter distressed the neighbours.

16

Sunday was not a holy day at number 57 Beckett Street. Kasturbhai MacGregor had made a point of taking her children to Sunday school each week but Kasturbhai was no longer in residence. Jawaharlal and Emily lolled in bed with Simeon and Elizabeth wedged between them and felt no religious inspiration. The peace of the holiday street filtered in through the sagging cardboard Jawaharlal had taped across the broken windows. He sighed contentedly. What could go wrong on an English Sunday? Life was suspended, as though a truce had been signed. Who had ever heard of anything happening on a Sunday, of anyone being born or dying, of couples marrying or divorcing? If there was indeed a god he must surely be tied up all day answering all those prayers. Even the devil probably lounged in bed enjoying the *News of the World*. On a Sunday neither of them would bother to interfere with ordinary people like Jawaharlal MacGregor. His fate was briefly his own.

'Is good day for boozer,' he suggested happily.

'You enjoy yourself,' said Emily.

Unlike Satan Errol Taylor had ordered the heavy papers and he was concentrating on the arts sections, spurning the seductive rainbows of the colour supplements. There was a particularly impressive article on Robbe-Grillet. Errol was interested to learn of the existence of Robbe-Grillet and he found the critique impressive. He wondered what Mr Potter, the head librarian, would have made of it and he resolved to mention it the following morning.

Neither Georgia Shuttleworth nor Patrick Kew were much concerned at that particular moment with spiritual matters. It had been a restless night. 'My bed's a bit small for two,' he said.

'It's really time you came up to my room,' she said. 'I've got a double.'

Owen Davies fumbled for his watch, rolled over and anticipated opening time.

Godfrey Thackeray scanned the papers, tracking down the weekend developments in the case of the Beast of Eastbourne, and thought about Owen Davies. It was time he pumped him — discreetly, of course — about the perplexing relationship between Faith Hope and the new tenant.

Only Mrs Prendergast observed a ritual that was appropriately devout. She no longer attended church regularly. Somehow the services had never seemed the same since that nasty Bishop of Woolwich. But she read the first chapter of the Revelation of St. John the Divine and derived particular comfort from the third verse: 'Blessed is he that readeth, and they that hear the words of this prophecy, and keep those things which are written therein: for the time is at

163

hand.'

'Do you hear that, Henry?' she inquired. 'The time is at hand. The prophecy is about to be fulfilled.'

Trade may have been sluggish in the front pews of the church of All Saints but it promised to be brisk in the three bars of the King Arthur public house. At noon a cluster of the faithful assembled outside its locked doors. At thirty seconds past noon Owen Davies was pounding a fist on frosted glass. 'Open up, bach,' he called. 'Is this or is this not the sort of hostelry where a man can purchase beer? Must we all die of thirst on the very edge of the oasis?' At his side Godfrey Thackeray rubbed his arms against the cold and pretended not to notice. Godfrey was not a practising drinking man.

Clad in Sunday sweaters and weekend bonhomie the regulars drifted in. Within half an hour the counters were heavily populated and the doors marked *KNIGHTS* and *DAMSELS IN DISTRESS* were in business. In the Lancelot Lounge a trim young man in cavalry twills leaned across a lager and lime to smile at a girl with a face that suggested regret. In the Guinevere Snuggery a middle-aged couple sat before glasses of Guinness and silently appraised separate suits of armour. In the Excalibur Bar an old man licked beer from his moustache and witnessed Godfrey Thackeray's investment in a pint of bitter and a gin and tonic.

'Well, isn't this nice,' said Godfrey.

Owen lifted his glass. 'God bless you, boyo,' he said.

164

Georgia stood at Kew's window smoking a cigarette and taking stock of the street. A child was kicking a football against a garden gate. Each time the ball clanked against the gate it rattled the latch. Thud clank rattle. Thud clank rattle. Across the street, at the kerb, a man was washing a car. With an assortment of buckets and cloths he splashed, foamed, rinsed and burnished the car. Thud clank rattle. Thud clank rattle. A cry of protest, an angry woman's voice. Thud clank rattle. The woman's voice again. The street went quiet. Georgia could almost hear the windscreen squeak as the man punished it. He polished energetically, now and then retreating for approval. He flicked a speck from the bonnet. It began to rain.

'I think I love you,' she said.

She drew deeply on the cigarette, trapping the smoke a long while in her lungs and streaming it gently from her nostrils. Across the road the man scurried round the car hunting for drops of rain as they splattered the roof and exterminating them with vigour. A dog sloped by seeking shelter and shaking its head.

'Did you hear what I said?'

'Yes.'

The rain eased and the dog stopped, looking back over its shoulder, reviewing the situation. She turned from the window to face him. He was shaving, bending at the basin in a pair of jeans and peering into the mirror.

'I like watching you shave.'

'Why?'

'I don't know. It's just . . . good.'

Her lips played with smoke. She watched him as he leaned forward, squinting, scraping his chin. 'Are you glad?' she said.

'What?'

'Glad.'

'What about?'

'What I said. You know.'

He bowed low over the basin, splashing the soap from his face and wiping it dry with a towel. 'You don't know me.'

'That's not my fault.'

'You don't know anything about me.'

'So?'

'I could be anyone.'

'But you're not. You're you.' He draped the towel over the edge of the basin and reached for his shirt. 'I love you as you are.'

He tugged his shirt over his head.

'Don't you believe me?'

He tucked the shirt into his jeans, smoothing his hair, looking away from her. 'I don't want to believe you,' he said.

She reached forward for the ashtray and murdered her cigarette. She turned and looked out of the window, leaning on outstretched arms. A family was walking home from church, the children scampering ahead, the parents sure in the knowledge of duty well done.

'Patrick, are you afraid of me?'

'Of course not.'

'Are you afraid of yourself?'

166

He stretched into a sweater and positioned himself at the mirror, combing his hair.

'Is it another girl?'

He hesitated. 'No.'

He pressed the last tuft of wayward hair into place. She walked across and hugged him. She kissed him. 'I understand,' she said.

He broke away gently to find his jacket.

'Where are you going?'

'The pub.'

She smiled. 'Oh, good. I could do with a drink.'

'No.'

'Mmmm?'

'I'm sorry. Not today. I need to be alone.' She frowned and opened her mouth. 'Sometimes I need to be alone.'

She smiled. 'Of course, darling. I understand. I'll see you later.'

In the hall, by the front door, she kissed him again. 'Don't be late,' she said. 'I'm doing something special for lunch.'

Errol Taylor had devised for himself a new Sunday routine. He would set his alarm for 8.30 and absorb the significant sections of the quality newspapers. At midday he would venture out for an hour's constitutional. He had discovered that John Kennedy had believed that the mind could not possibly function at its peak without proper physical exercise, and what was good enough for J.F.K. was good enough for Errol Flynn Taylor. If he walked for an hour at four miles per hour he would return toned up for a long

167

afternoon and evening of study. He felt it gave his life new purpose.

He had walked towards the park and had stopped to watch a game of football. It had not detained him long. The players seemed to be more concerned with yelling abuse at each other than with scoring goals. At the near end the goalkeeper leaned against one of his posts smoking a pipe. His left back sprawled at the touchline with one arm wrapped round a girl's waist and the other brandishing a bottle of beer. The ball itself appeared to be bogged down in mud at the far end, surrounded by vocal players barging each other and hacking wildly. The worst offender was a man in a cloth cap, blue windcheater and green trousers smeared with mud. A girl with a massive chest and a whistle was attempting to referee. Errol wiped his nose on his sleeve and continued his journey. What an infantile way to spend a Sunday morning.

After exactly half an hour he turned and walked back, arranging a detour to avoid the hubbub in the park. As he stretched his stride along Beckett Street he saw the new tenant coming towards him.

'Good morning, Mr Kew,' said Errol.

'Hullo.'

'No, I tell a lie. It's good afternoon, really, isn't it?'

'I suppose it is.'

'Are you out for your constitutional? There's nothing like a constitutional, I always say.'

'I'm going to the pub, actually.'

'Ah, well. All work and no play makes Jack a dull boy.' Errol laughed confidently. 'But it's back to Robbe-Grillet for me. The French novelist, you know. Or rather, anti-novelist.'

'Yes, I know.'

Errol stabbed at his glasses. 'You know Robbe-Grillet?'

'Well . . .'

Errol's nose twitched. 'Have you read any of his books?'

'A couple.'

'That's fascinating.' Errol inspected his watch. Surely he could spare half an hour? 'Look,' he said, 'do you mind if I join you? In the pub?'

'Well . . .'

'Perhaps we could have a bite.'

'I really . . .'

'I'd love to talk to you about Robbe-Grillet. It's not often you find a fellow spirit. I could do with a good discussion. We're a bit short on intellectuals around here, don't you find? Or perhaps you're meeting someone?'

'No. Not really.'

'Oh well. In that case. You can't sit drinking on your own, can you? First sign of alcoholism, that. Come on, let me buy you a half. Now, what about Robbe-Grillet? What do you feel about his reputed inhumanity?'

When they reached the King Arthur Errol insisted on drinking in the Lancelot Lounge. 'Not the Excalibur,' he said. 'They're not our sort in there. Not our sort at all.'

Bunched together in the Excalibur Bar Owen Davies, Godfrey Thackeray and Jawaharlal MacGregor were

169

united in a scene of good fellowship. Godfrey was in fact beginning to question whether the fellowship was perhaps a little too good.

For each gin and tonic he had consumed Owen Davies had engulfed a pint of bitter. At first Godfrey had encouraged this swift intake. Indeed, after a couple of pints Owen Davies had felt quite free to discuss his relationship with Georgia Shuttleworth. 'Not a bad screw, boyo,' he had announced, 'but a man doesn't want to get stuck in the same groove for ever, like, does he now?' Godfrey had considered this to be a significant development since it indicated that Faith Hope was perhaps less innocent than he had been led by the first couple of chapters to suppose. Even with her faint trace of moustache it appeared that her other attributes — long blonde hair, long slim legs, etc. — had led her into wickedness. After his third gin Godfrey did not consider this to be a bad thing. Somehow he did not feel that the time was right for a wholly virtuous heroine. But the trouble with Owen Davies was that he declined to stick to his facts. After his second pint he had stressed that a man could not be expected to endure too many nights with the same woman. After his third he had alluded to female fickleness. By the time he was into his fourth the little Indian had joined them and Owen Davies was becoming vehement in his denunciation of filthy whores in general and of the new tenant in particular.

Godfrey found all this bewildering. Owen Davies, expansive with Worthington E, had been buying drinks for several other regulars as well and the group began to enlarge. Smoke drifted hot across his face and strange men were telling dubious jokes and gins and tonics Godfrey had never anticipated seemed to be breeding on the counter before his eyes. There were three there now, squatting low and lethal in a row, and an Australian voice was urging him to stop dragging the chain.

'No more,' said Godfrey. 'No. Please. I have plenty.' And then there where four.

'Sink them, boyo.'

'You're cluttering up the bar.'

'Knock knock. Go on, you've got to ask who's there. Knock knock.'

'Who's there?'

'Gestapo.'

'Gestapo who?'

'Silence! Ve vill ask ze questions.'

Towards closing time Godfrey leaned across and plucked Owen Davies by the sleeve. 'You know?' he said. 'Mr Davies,' he said. 'You know he's a murderer? You know that, don't you? The Beast of Eastbourne. The Beast.'

'God save us, Thackers, bach. You've just time to buy another round, see.'

They were the last to leave, the landlord bustling round them emptying ashtrays and muttering. Jawaharlal MacGregor was giggling. 'Oh my God,' he said. 'Is too damn fine.' Godfrey peered at them, puckering up his eyes. Owen and two of his friends stood together singing, waving their beer glasses and recounting the sorry saga of The Ball of Kirriemuir.

On the pavement they said farewell to the rattle of

the landlord's bolts, pledging comradeship and prom-
ising reunions. Godfrey Thackeray and Owen Davies
and Jawaharlal MacGregor stepped hopefully in the
direction of 57 Beckett Street.

As they creaked in through the gate Emily appeared at the door to the basement. She was crying.
'They've been again,' she said.

17

Jawaharlal MacGregor ushered Owen Davies and Godfrey Thackeray away. He did not want another conference in the basement that might force him to inform the police. 'Is nothing at all,' he said. 'Is purely personal matter. I am now knowing course of action. Is nothing but domestic tribulations.'

As Emily and the children had cowered inside the flat vandals had delivered a letter through the door and bricks through four more windows. Two Indians, she had said, young boys, not more than seventeen or eighteen. 'Bloody nephews,' guessed Jawaharlal.

He studied the letter. It had been typed on a crippled machine. 'From the Desk of G.K. Bhave (Graduate),' it announced, 'Legal Expert, Property and Modern Philosopher.' Jawaharlal was horribly impressed.

TO WHOMSOEVER IT MAY CONCERN, GOD SAVE THE QUEEN

Sir,

I am in receipt of Certain Informations in my capacity as Legal Consultant to the Discerning Classes of this Metropolis via a certain Esteemed Lady to whit your esteemed not to say gracious Spouse my sister KASTURBHAI MACGREGOR (née Bhave).

Such communications from the aforesaid and aforementioned Lady, whom I find in Distressed Conditions, touch upon sundry delicate not to say intimate matters of Conjugal Rights, Obligations, Etc.

Mr MacGregor, sir, whereas such unfortunate Informations appear to have certain basis in Fact, to whit:

(1) it is Alleged you have wilfully and with Malice Afore-thought withdrawn the aforesaid and aforementioned Comforts, Duties, Etc. to which you are obliged under the Marriage Contract to provide withal to the aforesaid and afore-mentioned esteemed and gracious Lady your Spouse;

(2) it is Alleged you have wilfully and with Utter Disregard for the provisions of the aforesaid and aforementioned Contract inflicted financial, monetary and practical discomforts not only upon your Lady Spouse but also upon your Delightful Family, to whit the delicate matter of provisioning Necessities of Life to the following
   (a) Master JAGDISH MACGREGOR
   (b) Master RAJIV MACGREGOR
   (c) Miss INDIRA MACGREGOR

174

To their Certified Detriment and to the Unlawful not to say Criminal Advantage of the below-mentioned Infants Unlawfully and Carnally brought forth without due sanction of Church or State, e.g. (a) one SIMEON JACKSON, (b) a certain ELIZABETH JACKSON, being bastards of your loins and those of a woman by name EMILY JACKSON (née Jackson);

(3) Whereas it is further Alleged that this Woman aforesaid and aforementioned not only habits with you but cohabits to such a degree that it is alleged She is once again In Flagrante Delicto despite Numberous Entreaties and Express Wishes urged continually by the aforesaid and aforementioned Lawful and Loving Spouse to whit my sister KASTURBHAI MACGREGOR (née Bhave) a Lady of Esteemed and Gracious Nature not to mention her Position as your Legal Spouse, sir.

THEREFORE be it understood that the Aforesaid and Aforementioned Matters being duly considered by me in my Capacity as Graduate of Many Universities and Legal Consultant to the Discerning Classes of this Metropolis and upon Due Authority vested therein by the said Esteemed and Gracious Lady your Spouse that this be taken, understood, considered and vouched for as a Perfectly Legal and Binding WARNING: viz. unless Immediate Steps are put in motion (1) To rid your Present Household of the said Woman Jackson and the said Unlawful and Carnal Bastards; (2) Due Restitution be made to restore to their Rightful Comforts and Constitutional Security the aforesaid and aforementioned Legal Spouse your wife my sister KASTURBHAI MACGREGOR (née Bhave) together and in company with her Legal and Delightful Children of your body lawfully conceived and executed:
BE IT KNOWN, sir, that certain unpleasant Legal Procedures would then need to be Considered, Weighed and Activated for the aforesaid and aforementioned Conditions to be fulfilled.

175

Dated above my Hand this day, I am, sir, your humble and obedient servant.

God Save the Queen.

Yours faithfully,

G.K. BHAVE Esq. (GRADUATE).

'What does it mean?' asked Emily.

Jawaharlal rubbed his nose. 'Goddammit, I am not understanding hardly even one word.'

'It's from a lawyer.'

'Of course is from lawyer. Is from brother-in-law G.K. Bhave who is lawyer. That much is obvious.'

'Perhaps she wants a divorce. That's what lawyers are for, isn't it?'

'Is no mention of divorce. Is not one syllable on subject of divorce.'

'Well, why else should they want a lawyer?'

Jawaharlal pondered. 'I am needing advice.'

'Lawyers are expensive, mister.'

'Is no need for lawyer. After lunch I am consulting Dr Patrick.'

'Him?'

'Is man of education.' Jawaharlal nodded. 'Dr Patrick will be understanding.'

Emily turned on the radio as they ate their Sunday lunch. Simeon and Elizabeth bounced in their chairs to the music. They had accepted already the departure of Kasturbhai and her three children and were excited by their new importance. Jawaharlal smiled and leaned across the table to fuzz his daughter's hair. But the breeze blew sharp from the broken window. He shivered and felt afraid.

The new tenant sat alone in his room and understood what he had to do.

She had chided him when he returned from the pub. 'It's a special celebration. You nearly ruined the meal.' And then she had offered him wine and comfort, warm and all-enveloping in the drowsy afternoon.

After lunch he had escaped. But first they had cleared up together, she with a brush and he with a cloth. The suds sparkled bright in the basin and he glowed the plates with shining at her side. 'It's almost like being married,' she had said.

Yes. Like that late summer evening on the beach with Mary. It had been cold but the air had been warm by contrast and the roughness of their towels after the water had left them excited. They had picked their way across the rocks, scuffing the sand and rinsing their toes in warm, shallow pools. The night had crept up the beach with the tide, the white surge of the waves isolating them on a hillock of beach above the water line. Beneath the massive patronage of the cliff they had whispered nakedly.

He pressed his eyes with the heels of his hands, recreating the pinpoint stars against the blackness of that night. Poor Mary. Poor, sweet Mary. 'Mine, mine,' she had whispered. 'For ever.' How can you suffer claustrophobia at night on an endless beach beneath an open sky? Forgive me, Georgia. Forgive me for what I must do. Here, perhaps, within these cramped walls, I have more excuse.

Georgia Borgia,
Pudding and pie,
Kissed the boys and made them cry.

Forgive me, Georgia. It has to be done. You make demands and I have no answers. I am inadequate.

Jawaharlal discovered him sunk in his chair. Outside the afternoon was tidying itself away.

'I am disturbing?'

'Not at all. Come in.'

Jawaharlal closed the door. 'I am needing advice, Dr Patrick.'

He shook his head gently. 'Sit down,' he said. 'Look, Mr MacGregor, I'm not a doctor. I've told you. I used to be a medical student, that's all. I'm just plain Patrick Kew, not Dr Patrick.'

Jawaharlal settled nervously on the edge of a chair. 'You are man of education. I am not understanding such things. I am worried man, Dr Patrick. Goddammit, yes.'

'What's the matter?'

He listened quietly to Jawharlal's report, from his heated description of the infamy of the woman from Bombay to his bewilderment at the letter from G.K. Bhave.

'What is meaning, Dr Patrick? What is woman wanting?'

Kew examined the letter. 'It seems she wants to come back to you. She wants you to herself, alone.'

'Is impossible. Goddammit, this woman is not loving me. She is merely wanting vacant possession.'

178

Kew said nothing. It seemed there was nothing to say.

'What am I doing, Dr Patrick? Emily is frightened. They are smashing windows. Is intolerable. The children. And now is letters from lawyers. What is man like me doing with lawyers, are you answering that?'

Kew returned the letter. 'Why don't you go and see your wife? Have it out with her. Come to some settlement. You could tell her that if there's any more trouble you'll send for the police.'

'No, no, not police.'

'They can't just smash your windows whenever they feel like it.'

'No, Dr Patrick. Not police. I am Indian, you are understanding. Is always problem with police.'

'Well, I'd go and see her, anyway.'

'*You* will be seeing her?'

'No, not me. You. If I were *you* I'd go and see her.'

'Yes, yes. Is excellent idea. Please, you are seeing her with me?'

'Me?'

'Oh yes, indeed. I am needing assistance, Dr Patrick.'

'That's impossible. This is a matter between you and your wife. This is private. It's got nothing to do with me.'

Jawaharlal was pleading, his hands measuring air. 'Is private? Is private with lawyers and family with bricks through windows? How am I dealing with lawyers, Dr Patrick? I am simple man. I am not even understanding letter. You are understanding letter.

You are speaking with lawyer, you are understanding provocations.'

There was silence. Kew interlocked his fingers, resting his chin on his knuckles. 'I'm sorry,' he said. 'It's out of the question.'

Jawaharlal leaned back in his chair and scratched in his pocket for a handkerchief. Tears advanced quietly over the crest of his cheeks. He dabbed at his eyes. 'Please be excusing,' he said. 'I am sorry for such behaviour.' He rose and nodded briefly, blinking, hurrying to the door.

How could he refuse this man? How could he sit before his fire untouched by his misery? 'Where is your wife?'

Jawaharlal turned at the door. 'I am thinking with brother-in-law, with Bhave lawyer.'

'Where's that?'

'About five mile.'

Kew stood up. 'All right. I'll come. But we'll have to go now.'

'Now?'

'I may not be able to do it tomorrow.'

Jawaharlal MacGregor wiped his eyes and came across to shake the hand of Patrick Kew.

Georgia curled on her bed watching the branches fade against the darkening sky. How long had she known him? It did not matter. Already she found herself becoming jealous of his independence. She resented each separate minute they ought to be together. Even now he was only a few feet beneath her, sitting solitary no doubt in front of that damned fire. So he

180

needed to be alone. How long did he want? An hour, two, three? Would he return or should she go down and jettison all pride? And if so, when? Now, later, tomorrow? To hell with him, she thought. If he wants me he knows where to find me.

At regular intervals throughout the afternoon and early evening she referred to her watch.

It was becoming too dark to read without a lamp and to switch it on Errol would have to move from his seat. He frowned, dissatisfied. He was troubled by his concentration. Several times during the afternoon he had turned pages and could not recollect their message. He had had to go back and force himself with his finger to follow the paragraphs.

He knew it had been a mistake going to the pub with Patrick Kew. It had disturbed his purpose. Errol blinked, irritated. He had not enjoyed Kew's company. The man had apparently read several of Robbe-Grillet's works and considered them point-less. Superficial, he had said. Sterile, he had said. He had also made alarming references to some woman called Nathalie Sarraute, of whom Errol had never heard. Errol had felt suspicious about the intro-duction of this red herring into the conversation and on their return had sought out his Dictionary of Modern Literature. There it had been – Nathalie Sarraute, another ruddy anti-novelist. Kew was quite definitely an aggravation.

Errol squinted down at the shadowed page. It squatted on his lap, solid and uninviting. Drat Kew.

He looked across at his bed. It sprawled sideways,

still unmade. Across it, crumpled, lay the weary grey pages of the quality Sunday papers. He snapped the book shut and tossed it onto the table. He made the bed and stood disgruntled at the window brooding over fallen leaves. Then he drew the curtains, switched on the lamp and settled down to read the colour supplements. After all, one had to keep an open mind. There might be some very stimulating, intellectual stuff in the colour supplements.

Errol grunted and poked his glasses up his nose. He could not imagine Kew studying the pages of colour supplements. Arrogant know-all.

Every weekday the late Henry Prendergast was obliged to listen to his wife but on Sunday evenings came his chance to reply. Mrs Prendergast no longer felt it necessary to attend the evening service since the Church was now quite patently in league with the Prince of Darkness and in any case she had no further need of external spiritual inspiration. She no longer required priestly callisthenics to keep the muscle of her soul in trim. Instead, on Sunday evenings, she would disclose her ouija-board and set it on the table by the window. For Henry's benefit she would arrange her hair and stroke a little lipstick round her mouth. True, he had taken little notice of her appearance while he had been alive but it was possible that people changed for the better when they crossed the eternal barrier into the Great Beyond.

Henry certainly seemed to have changed, but whether it was for the better Mrs Prendergast did not feel entitled to judge. Not only did he direct her hand to the oddest sections of the Bible for her daily text but he had recently taken to posing riddles during their Sunday evening conversations on the ouija-board. Last Sunday his communication had read PORKWQTESTFRAGSY. It had taken several hours to work that one out and even then she was not entirely satisfied. Asssuming that Henry's spelling had deteriorated a little and that he was also using abbreviations she had translated the message to read 'Poor K.W. quietest for ages. Why?' K.W. was obviously Katharine Wilson, whose death seven years ago had successfully silenced the staunchest voice in the Women's Institute. It was certainly of interest to discover that since her death Katharine had simmered down, but why could Henry not have reported it in a simpler fashion? It was always possible that Henry was just too lazy to spell out the complete message, but to be charitable Mrs Prendergast suspected that the inhabitants of the Great Beyond found it extremely wearying to operate the ouija-board. After all, if they had no bodies the effort must sap their mental energies abominably. Mrs Prendergast understood such matters and accordingly restricted her two-way conversations to Sunday evenings.

She organized herself at the table, hair neat, lips tinted, dressed in her best cardigan and skirt. The light was on in the room across the road and the parrot stared disconsolately toward her. Mrs Prendergast waved at the parrot and drew the curtains. In the dark she closed her eyes, resting her hands on the table. For ten minutes she would manicure her mind of evil influences. Evil influences could conjure up unwanted demons. She had read somewhere that people with nasty minds had found themselves on such occasions clutching at the brink of Hell with sulphurous flames toying with their feet. Mrs Prendergast was not prepared to take such risks. As insurance she crossed herself three times and delivered the Lord's Prayer. Then she addressed herself to the Unseen and requested the presence of Henry Charles Prendergast, deceased, formerly of 19 Nasturtium Villas, and waited.

Ten minutes later Mrs Prendergast's right hand began to tremble. 'Are you there, Henry?' she inquired. Her hand trembled again. 'You're late,' she said. 'What kept you so long?'

Urged by irresistible powers her hand reached for the pointer and began to move it round the ouija-board. The pointer rested at V. Then it moved on to S and stopped.

'V. S.?' said Mrs Prendergast.

Her hand trembled.

V.S.? Veterinary Surgeon? Surely not. No, there couldn't possible by any animals Over There. V. S. Verse? Henry writing verse? No – no, that was ridiculous. Henry's ether was unlikely even now to be of a poetic nature. Perhaps he meant he had been reading a verse in the Bible.

V. S., registered Mrs Prendergast, suddenly appalled. Vera Simpson.

'Henry! What have you been doing with Vera Simpson?'

Her hand moved again, selecting the letters around the board. It moved to G and C and F and R and K

and D. GCFRKD? G cough are code? GKF raked?
Gec forked?

'What is this, Henry?' Her hand lay still. 'Are you
tired, Henry?' Her hand shook slightly. She sighed.
'All right, Henry. Do you have any message for me
this week?'

Wearily the pointer circled the board. Each time it
hesitated Mrs Prendergast noted the adjacent letter on
the pad at her side. TMNUSKSNTCMNG, remarked
her husband. TMNUSKSNTCMNG.

It had taken a long time, the letters laboriously
picking themselves out around the board. Mrs Prendergast felt very tired. She relaxed and closed her
eyes. Henry was gone. It was always like this at the
end. His chilly fatigue seemed to infect her even
across the barriers of alien worlds.

After a while she roused herself to make a cup
of tea and decipher the message. TMNUSK-
SNTCMNG. Time news kiss . . . no. Terminus K sent
coming. No, T minus K sent, come in G.

What?

Mrs Prendergast sat and stirred her tea, sat and
drank her tea, sat and consulted the leaves at the
bottom of the cup. Long after they were cold and
with several sheets of paper lying crumpled on the
table she found herself in possession of one sentence
that appeared to make sense.

'The man you seek,' it said, 'isn't coming.'

Mrs Prendergast read it several times and shook
her head, annoyed. 'Nonsense, Henry,' she said.
'You're up to your tricks again.'

Godfrey Thackeray had slept for a couple of hours following his research in the Excalibur Bar of the King Arthur public house. He awoke to a general seediness of body and sogginess of mind. He hated Sunday afternoons. On weekdays, with everyone else at work, he could tap all day at his typewriter without noticeable ill-effects. At the weekend it required a special effort of will.

He had forced himself over to his desk and had attempted to distil his new knowledge into prose. After his conversation with Owen Davies he now allowed Faith Hope to make full use of her long blonde hair, long slim legs and firm, uptilted organs. He permitted his fictional Welshman to enjoy these attributes before abandoning Faith for a barmaid.

So far so good. But Godfrey tussled long with the problem of the strange young killer living on the ground floor. He progressed warily, carefully concocting a paragraph and sitting back to think. Obviously the killer wanted Faith as a new victim, and artistically it would be perfect if Faith should herself be the unsuspecting instrument in determining her own ghastly fate. Ideally she should force herself on the young man, tempting him beyond endurance. But would that ever happen in real life? Godfrey doubted it. Would a girl like Faith with a faint trace of moustache on her upper lip ever find the self-confidence to force herself onto a man? And surely she would find such a man distasteful. There was bound to be a shiftiness about his eyes, a menacing suppleness about his fingers. Do girls fall for sex maniacs?

186

Godfrey worried over the puzzle. He just did not know enough about the man. Distasteful and dangerous as it might be he would have to accost Kew alias Lowry and learn more about him.

Godfrey adjusted his television set to catch the evening news and shuddered at his audacity. His courage impressed him. Here, in this very house, there skulked a brutal killer on the run and he, Godfrey Makepeace Thackeray, was undeterred. He chewed his fingers. It was a heck of a risk.

The newsreader's face flickered into view, urgent with its own importance. It was succeeded by a map of South East Asia, a view of the White House and a glimpse of a film star climbing out of a Rolls Royce.

'In the Eastbourne murder case police are still looking for Charles John Lowry, whom they believe can help them in their inquiries.' Godfrey leaned forward. On the screen there appeared an Identikit picture of the wanted man. 'Today the dead girl's employer, Mr Frederick Thomas, offered a £500 reward for information leading to the killer's arrest.

'In the Middle East . . .'

Godfrey gazed at a map of Israel. £500! That was five times what he had made out of *His Own Sweet Will.* Good grief, £500!

For at least half an hour Godfrey battled with his conscience. Surely it was his duty to tell the police. It was all very well going on about Art and Culture but there were lives at stake. How could he know whether Lowry would kill again? How could he accept such a responsiblity? Good gracious, Lowry might very well be planning right now to murder Georgia Shuttleworth just as Godfrey had already foreseen in the book. Did any artist have the right to place his genius before another human life and the collective security of society? Heavens, Lowry might even be responsible for the disappearance of Mac-Gregor's Indian wife.

These and other questions troubled Godfrey Thackeray. At length he clad himself in his overcoat and for protection he armed his pocket with his kitchen knife. Quietly unlocking his door he crept downstairs, taking care to tiptoe across the hall to the front door.

Once out in the street he walked swiftly towards the telephone box on the corner. He knew now that he had made the correct — the only — decision. This time there could be no turning back.

18

Emily had been subdued before they left. Jawaharlal could sense that she did not want him to go to speak to Kasturbhai. There was about her an aura of foreboding. Perhaps she was embarrassed by Dr Patrick's involvement, but Jawaharlal felt it was more than that. He had tried to explain his need for an ally, for someone to counter the erudition of G.K. Bhave. 'Dr Patrick is like lawyer without expenses,' he pointed out. Emily had nodded, unconvinced. Perhaps she was worried about the legal consequences. Could they bring court orders, paternity suits, even send him to prison? Jawaharlal shivered. An acquaintance of Chandra had once been sent to prison for a year without understanding anything of his trial. 'Do not be worrying,' he assured Emily. 'I am returning pretty damn quick.' She had nodded again. Did she fear that he would be kidnapped or beaten up by his burly nephews? Or that they might return while he was away and demolish the house? 'Chin chin,' said Jawaharlal, encouragingly.

As they left she had run towards him, heavy,

ungainly, painfully lovable, and had hugged him tightly for a moment. Over her shoulder he had noticed Simeon and Elizabeth watching, impressed by such unaccustomed emotion.

On the bus he and the new tenant said little, strangers sitting hip to hip. As they approached their destination Jawaharlal became apprehensive, bracing himself for his confrontation with Kasturbhai. Was it really only yesterday that she had left? As the bus rumbled through the idle afternoon, rattling the shuttered, under-populated streets, he could feel her grip tightening. She was drawing him to her, clawing him closer. The female praying mantis devours her mate even as he vests her with new life.

They covered several hundred yards from the bus stop, discovering Bhave's house in the centre of a terraced row.

'You all right?'

Jawaharlal nodded glumly. The patch of front garden was thickly tangled, the outside wall crumbling. A rusty bicycle wheel sprouted grass between its spokes. The paint round the door leaned tired against the wall. A breeze excavated the street, gathering the hems of their coats and flapping them irritably against their legs. Jawaharlal looked up. The clouds drifted low and black. 'And now is rain,' he said.

They rang the bell and studied the coloured panes of glass in the door. A neighbour rested on his garden wall and watched. A child peeped, frightened, from a window. Jawaharlal had always feared his brother-in-law. The orderly discipline of Bhave's household combined with his booming self-confidence always reminded Jawaharlal of childhood and the quiet horrors of dark corners and adult eyes watching across a room.

Bhave opened the door. 'Yes? Jawaharlal!'

'Is I.'

'Indeed it is you, Jawaharlal. We are able to acquire such information for ourselves.' Somehow he managed to fill his doorway, his head held higher than his height demanded. He looked at Jawaharlal and at Patrick Kew and back at Jawaharlal. 'Three questions, however, occur immediately. These are respectively (a) surprise at your presence, (b) curiosity as to your intentions and (c) a desire to know the identity of your companion. Perhaps you would be so good as to clarify such questions.'

Jawharlal massaged his nose nervously. 'Is Dr Patrick.'

Kew offered his hand. 'Mr Bhave? Patrick Kew. I'm one of your brother-in-law's neighbours.'

G.K. Bhave investigated Kew's hand with suspicion and touched it briefly. 'How pleased to make your acquaintance, Dr Patrick Kew.'

Kew sighed. It would only complicate the issue.

'What is your capacity, Dr Kew?'

'Capacity?'

'In which capacity do we have the honour to welcome you to our humble abode?'

'Mr MacGregor asked me to come along.'

G.K. Bhave swivelled his eyes accusingly towards Jawaharlal. 'For what particular purpose, may we inquire?'

191

'Please?'

Bhave sighed. 'Under what design have you in-veigled Dr Kew to our residence?'

Jawaharlal looked at Kew.

'He wants to know why I'm here.'

'Oh, indeed. Now I am understanding. Is adviser. Is legal adviser,' said Jawaharlal with menace.

Bhave raised his eyebrows. 'You are Doctor of Law, Dr Kew?'

'Is Kew, see,' said Jawaharlal.

'Ah,' said Bhave, wary. 'Ah. Q.C.'

Jawaharlal MacGregor armed himself with ancient Highland cunning. 'Is highly educated gentleman,' he pressed. 'Is also judo black belt, Bhave. Is useful friend. Much accomplishment.'

Kew considered his feet. Bhave stepped slightly back. 'Indeed,' he said. 'This is a singular honour. Our residence is yours to command, Dr Kew. However, we should first be grateful to ascertain certain matters, to whit replies to the first two queries already pro-pounded, i.e. (a) the cause for our brother-in-law's presence here and (b) his intentions. We would further submit, sir, with every respect, that it might be considered inadmissible behaviour for a gentleman to materialize upon our doorstep accompanied on a Holy Day by his legal adviser. Perhaps you would be so good as to advise us of such.'

Emboldened, Jawaharlal stepped towards the door. 'Where is wife? Where is goddam woman?'

G.K. Bhave placed a restraining palm on his chest. 'Your esteemed lady wife is incommunicado.'

'Why are you not speaking bloody English, god-
192

dammit.'

'Kasturbhai is not here.'

'This I am not believing.'

A figure appeared in the darkened passage behind Bhave. It was Kasturbhai. 'Is that the drunk adulterer?' she called. 'Do I hear the filth MacGregor?'

'This I am not believing even more,' repeated Jawaharlal, 'for certain reasons.'

G.K. Bhave stepped aside. 'Perhaps in the circumstances you have better enter. Come, Dr Kew, we may consult in my chamber. We have a degree, you know, from several eminent educational establishments.'

'Filth,' said Kasturbhai. 'Blasphemer filth.'

'Goddammit, woman,' said Jawaharlal.

'This is, of course, most irregular,' remarked G.K. Bhave.

They were arranged at a table, Jawaharlal and Kasturbhai on opposing sides with Bhave and Kew beside them acting as seconds. The room was furnished with a crippled typewriter, a shelf of tattered books, a coloured photograph of the Queen, a framed document testifying herewith and herefrom to the intellectual calibre of G.K. Bhave Esquire (Graduate) and, in the corner, Jawaharlal MacGregor's 25-inch television set. This, announced Bhave, was his consulting chamber. The door had been closed for privacy but seven children jostled at the window, peering in from the safety of the back yard.

G.K. Bhave rose, ill at ease on his buttocks. He tucked his thumbs into the top of his trousers. 'As we were saying, this procedure is highly irregular.'

Jawaharlal glared at Kasturbhai. 'What is this throwing bricks through window?'

Bhave lifted a hand. 'Silence!'

'Is bricks through six window.'

Bhave appealed. 'Could you impress on your client, Dr Kew, the need for restraint?'

'Mr MacGregor. Shall we hear what Mr Bhave has to say?'

'Is likely to be all night.'

Bhave hooked his thumb in his trousers again. 'We shall ignore your client's interruptions,' he granted. 'As we were attempting to enunciate prior to his outburst, this is all highly irregular. We have, of course, been taken entirely unawares. We have had little time to prepare our brief. You will no doubt understand, Dr Kew, that in a household of Christian persuasion it is unusual to discover oneself concerned with matters of the Law on the Holy Day. Be that as it may and nem. con., so to speak, suffice it to be said that we shall of course attempt to discharge our utmost duty to our client in a manner befitting the dignity of our calling, not to mention our profound esteem for your good self. Perhaps we may best fulfil both tasks by recapitulating the sad, nay tragic, history of this sorry dispute. Seven years ago, as you are probably aware, our client arrived at these shores from her native land alone, bewildered, bereft and not to mention slightly apprehensive. She had no friends, no family, no comfort, no succour, no . . .'

Kew looked at his watch. 'I'm sorry, Mr Bhave. Forgive me for interrupting. But don't you think we could get straight to the point?'

'Dr Kew! This is most irregular.'

'I think the parties involved probably know the background already.'

'That has nothing whatever to do with the matter in hand, Dr Kew. We must establish a prima facie case. We must not rest from toil. We should not shirk our labours, Dr Kew, no, neither on the beaches nor in the fields. We shall . . .'

'What is bloody fool talking about?'

'You shut up, filth. Blasphemer.'

'Goddammit, woman, is patience I am losing.'

'Filth. Adulterer.'

Jawaharlal half rose from his chair. Kew tugged at his sleeve. G.K. Bhave waved his arms in the air. 'This is unconstitutional,' he cried. 'Dr Kew, please be good enough to control your client.'

Jawaharlal slumped back in his seat.

'Pig,' said Kasturbhai.

The day had surrendered, collapsing weakly behind the suburban roofs, before G.K. Bhave prepared to sit down. 'And that,' he announced, 'concludes the case for the prosecution. Quod erat demonstration, so to speak. May we simply add our apologies for the inadequacies of our humble talents for eloquence and crave the indulgence of the court.'

As he sat down, wiping his brow, Kasturbhai rested a hand on his arm. 'Brilliant,' she said. 'I do not understand how they have not made you a judge.'

Jawaharlal stirred uncomfortably. 'And I am not understanding one word. Dr Patrick, what is goddam

195

man saying? Please be telling.'

'He says your wife has left you because of Emily, and you must tell Emily to leave and then she will return to you.'

'Is all? Is no more?'

'That's about it.'

Jawaharlal appraised his brother-in-law and shook his head. 'Is remarkable man. Is taking one hour to be telling what I am already knowing. Is brilliant.'

Bhave frowned and prepared to rise to his feet.

'Thank you, Mr Bhave. I think we have the facts very clearly established now. We are all very grateful to you.'

G.K. Bhave smiled and shrugged. 'It is nothing. It is no more than our duty, Dr Kew.'

'Perhaps Mr MacGregor might now be allowed to reply.'

'Reply?'

'Yes.'

Bhave's eyes widened. 'But this is utterly irregular.'

'I'm sorry?'

'Such a procedure would be entirely without precedent.'

'I don't follow.'

'Surely, Dr Kew, surely. We cannot allow your client to speak for himself. It would completely destroy the dignity of this hearing. It is your duty to reply on behalf of your client. We cannot allow him to answer a case which we, who are practised in the procedure of the courts, have conducted at great personal tribulation, not to mention expense. Such a procedure would utterly undermine our position.

196

Surely you can see that, Dr Kew? Surely you can . . .'

'Of course. My apologies.'

'What is old windbag discussing now?' inquired Jawaharlal.

'Adulterer filth. Be shutting mouth, filth.'

'They want me to ask you some questions.'

Jawaharlal poked a finger at his wife. 'And is I am wanting to be asking questions also.'

'Just two questions. Are you going to tell Emily to leave?'

'Goddammit, no.'

'Second question. Do you want your wife back?'

Jawaharlal laughed sourly. 'Her?'

Kew faced G.K. Bhave. 'That seems to be the situation, then. Stalemate. I now have just one question to ask of you, Mr Bhave. What do you intend to do about it? Once that is established we can go.'

Kasturbhai was on her feet. 'Filth,' she said. 'You dirty, drunk, ignorant pig with your fat, ugly, black whore. I will teach you. You will pay for blasphemy, you pig. Filth. Impotent. You and that dirty black bitch. That dirty, ugly, fat black whore . . .'

No one could stop him. With a grunt Jawaharlal MacGregor shed his chair, taking three steps round the table and punching his wife in the eye. As she fell back he followed her, summoning up from some deep tribal memory of Lucknow or Bannockburn the courage to hit her again, in the mouth.

Then they were on him, clutching his arms, holding him back.

'Assault!' cried G.K. Bhave. 'Battery! Grievous

197

bodily harm!'

Kasturbhai cowered on the floor, her hands across her face, sobbing.

'Intent! Menaces! Attempted murder!'

Jawaharlal, restrained, looked down at her. 'I am warning you, woman,' he said quietly. 'I am warning you now for seven year.'

On the bus back to Beckett Street they travelled in silence, Jawaharlal nursing his knuckles. 'I am apologizing,' he said eventually. 'Is not manners to be showing you such behaviour, Dr Patrick.'

They rode for another mile, the only passengers aboard. 'Is possible I am going to prison?'

'I don't think so. I think a man is allowed to discipline his wife.'

Jawaharlal massaged the back of his hand and pondered the rain sparkling off the road into the gutters. 'I am ashamed,' he said. 'Is no way to be treating woman. Even wife. Is wrong.'

At the bus stop in Beckett Street they hoisted their collars against the weather, their footsteps sharp against the riffle of the rain.

'I'm sorry. I don't seem to have been much help.'

'Is my fault. Is very good to be helping. Is very kind.'

'Not at all.'

'Yes, yes. Is most kind. You are coming in for cup of tea?'

'No, no. Thanks all the same.'

'Yes, yes. I am insisting. Emily is wanting to be thanking you.'

'No, really. It's very kind of you but I've got a lot to do this evening.'

They stopped at the front door, sheltering in the porch. The rain splattered from the trees, sweeping suddenly round them and up against the door.

'I hope everything turns out all right.'

'I am having my Emily.'

'Yes.'

'Is no more I am wanting.'

'You're lucky.'

Jawaharlal smiled wanly. 'Is only now I am realizing.'

Down the stairs to the basement, huddled into his coat, Jawaharlal noticed the lights were all out. He felt a pain at the base of his throat. Emily!

The door was locked. When he had found his key and let himself in he understood even before he reached for the light switch that the flat was empty. It was so quiet he could hear Dr Patrick closing his door upstairs and creaking across the floorboards.

Jawaharlal switched the light on. 'Emily? Emily? *Emily*!'

For the first time ever he heard his neighbours through the party wall with number 59. A man was laughing.

19

Georgia heard his footsteps at the gate and listened
for his voice. She waited, checking her impulse to run
down to him. He would come. She knew he would
come, she willed him to come to her. Her heart
thumped foolishly, proving to her finally his power
over her. From now on he could do as he liked – she
vowed never to complain. What was her jealousy
worth if it came between them? He was more
important to her than her pride. What did it matter if
he sometimes wanted to be alone? What did it matter
if he sometimes left her so long as he was there to
return again? How had she ever imagined herself
happy with Owen? They were so different, Owen
cheerful and buoyant, Patrick quiet and dull – yes,
dull – and yet it was Patrick she needed. She would
try to learn. She would begin to learn tonight. No
matter how long it took she would wait. There must
be no more pushing, no insistence. She would let him
make the rules and she would obey them. For some
reason he was afraid and she would respect that fear.
One day she would understand but she would only

know because he wanted to tell. It would be difficult but she would try.

She heard him moving around in the room below and wondered when he would come. She would not ask him where he had been. But he would be cold and wet and would need a cup of coffee. She wanted to have one ready for him.

As she crossed the room she glimpsed herself in the oval mirror hanging above the mantelpiece. She examined her reflection. 'I love him,' she said.

Errol Taylor wandered restlessly around his room, leaning against the wall, peering out at the rain through the crack in the curtains, reading a paragraph in a newspaper and throwing it down again. Books littered the table. He took one, rubbing his finger across the lettering on the spine, and put it down again. The evening lay in heavy chunks around him. He dredged his nose with thoughtful industry. Tomorrow was Monday and Mr Potter and old men fingering *Lady Chatterley* and *Fanny Hill.* He thought of Georgia Shuttleworth and the way her mouth twitched attractively at the corners when she smiled, like that girl in the last issue of *Playboy.* He was looking for the magazine when he heard a key in the front door, the click of the lock as it closed again and footsteps across the hall. Another door opened and closed. Errol pressed his glasses firmly into the base of his forehead. That Patrick Kew. Pompous twit.

The King Arthur was always quiet on a Sunday night.

The lunchtime regulars stayed at home, their week-end joviality evaporating with the promise of Monday morning. The landlord leaned on the counter judging the pin-ups in the *Sunday Mirror*. He hummed to himself. In the empty bar of the Guinevere Snuggery a suit of armour stood guard against the windy night.

Even Owen Davies was slow with his pint at the end of the counter in the Excalibur Bar. A brace of ladies topped with felt hats exchanged information over glasses of brown ale.

'Cold, innit?'

'Wet, too.'

'Yers.'

'Almost winter.'

'Cold, though, for the time of year.'

'Wet, too.'

'Yers.'

'It's them astronauts.'

'Like as not.'

'Messin' about.'

'Yers.'

'The moon, I mean.'

'Yers.'

'Them men on the moon.'

'Shouldn't be allowed. Fiddlin' about an' that.'

'Criminal, that's what it is. Criminal.'

Owen Davies investigated the froth on the top of his beer. He wrapped his hand around the glass. It was cold and hard to the touch. The curtains across the window shivered in a breeze. The door of the Lancelot Lounge creaked and a portly man advanced on the landlord, soliciting rums and ginger. His companion, a middle-aged woman with tinted hair, settled on a stool at the counter and crossed her legs with practised assurance. She smiled at Owen across the well of the bar.

'Good evening,' she said.

The man turned and nodded.

'Evening,' said Owen. He drew his finger through a drop of beer and created fantasies on the surface of the counter. That bastard Kew.

Mongoose should be here now, Mongoose perched provocatively at the bar, laughing at his jokes. They had always enjoyed the lull of Sunday evenings in the Arthur, the peaceful requiem for another week. They would smile, pretend, touch, feed the one-armed bandit. They would never drink too much on a night like this but would scurry early home, wrapped close, to lie together warm and listen to the rain rap rhythmically against the window pane. God damn that bastard Kew.

Owen stirred himself and swallowed deep from his pint. He wiped his lips. The foam lay thin and yellow at the bottom. He looked at his watch. Bloody hours to go. 'Same again, please, Fred.'

The portly man consulted the woman and called across the bar. 'Care to join us?' A nasty piece of work. Thin lips, wet mouth. 'Make up a party. Liven the place up a bit.'

Owen shrugged and slipped off his stool. Why not? 'Sure,' he said.

Jawaharlal MacGregor sat alone and scrutinized Emily's note. 'She is your wife,' it said. 'It is only rite. Dont foller me I'll look after your babies but dont try to find me. Dont feel sade for me I'll be alrite. Love, your Emily. P.S. Simeon and Elizabeth send love.'

He could hear the neighbours quite clearly now through the wall. A man was trying to shout above the noise of a television set. A tap was dripping firmly into the bath and he walked through to squeeze it shut. He coughed and the curve of the bath coughed hollowly back. His knuckles were beginning to swell and throb.

He wandered into the children's bedroom. She had made the bed before leaving. On the top of the chest of drawers there was a dust-free patch where Elizabeth's teddy bear had sat for days unwanted, frowning at the world.

He lay on his bed and pressed his nose into the pillow, smelling Emily. The cardboard flapped loose in the broken window, soft with the rain. Why had he gone and left her alone? He should have realized something like this might happen. Why had he bothered with Kasturbhai? To hell with Kasturbhai. He should never have listened to Dr Patrick. What did he know about his feelings, his love for Emily? He was white and educated and free. What did he understand of life in a London Transport uniform at a ticket barrier?

He would never find her now. Emily was not the sort of woman to come back. She would disappear into some teeming tenement and in four months give birth to a Jackson. She would remember him, yes. She would see him each day in the caramel faces of her children and she would remember. But for a woman like Emily he was already history, no more than another little tear to add to the ancient anguish of her race.

He smothered his face in the pillow, moistening the last lingering traces of her love. He thought briefly of Dr Patrick and his suggestion of gin and hot water and he cursed him for it.

At the top of the house, eavesdropping on the chuckle of rain along the gutters, Mrs Prendergast made a momentous decision.

Perhaps Henry's garbled message had been right after all. Perhaps he was not coming. If so Mrs Prendergast was not going to allow herself to be robbed so easily of her prophecy. If a heathen like Mohammed had had it in him to go to his mountain Mrs Prendergast felt it should not be beyond her.

She took comfort from the sensible ticking of the clock. 'Don't be shocked, Henry,' she said. 'I shall go to him myself. In the morning I shall make myself known.' The wind brushed noisily against the window pane, trembling the frame. 'In the morning, Henry,' said Mrs Prendergast primly.

On the other side of the top floor landing Godfrey Thackeray no longer deemed it necessary to lock his door. He sat with the pages of his novel in his lap. Methodically he tore each page in half and in half again, fluttering the scraps into the wastepaper basket at his side. On the desk his typewriter stood awkwardly silent.

They had been very polite. They had thanked him kindly for his trouble. 'It was very good of you to call, sir,' the policeman had told him over the phone. 'We very much appreciate it.'

Later, on the television news, it was announced that a Charles John Lowry had that evening presented himself at a police station in Cornwall and was now assisting in certain inquiries.

When Godfrey had destroyed the manuscript he pressed the pieces carefully into the bottom of the basket and set it down in its usual place beside the desk. He covered the typewriter and cleared away the loose scraps of paper, newspaper cuttings, folders and ballpoint pens, hiding them neatly in the drawer. He drew out the shiny paper-knife they had given him as a farewell present when he left the bank and tapped it lightly against his fingers. Would they give him his job back? There was probably some bright youngster there now with a smooth, round face and two A-levels. But Godfrey knew he had been useful. Mr Williams had stopped by his desk twice in that last week and had told him so. Perhaps he should write to him and sound him out. Discreetly, of course, just to see how the land lay. It would be good to be back in harness, good to experience again the stimulus of regular discipline. Not that he would give up his writing. Good Lord, no. He would write in the evenings. Well, at weekends, anyway. He might even take up a little golf again, the occasional gentle round on a Sunday afternoon. The fresh air would do him good. Life would be civilized again. There were certainly some very strange people in a place like this.

20

Jawaharlal MacGregor left for the early shift before dawn.

Later, late as usual on a Monday morning, Owen Davies and Errol Taylor had to sprint to catch their buses.

Georgia Shuttleworth stood quietly for a while in the hall outside Patrick's door. He seemed to be asleep. She smiled, hitching her bag over her shoulder. He would come up to see her this evening, she knew. She would buy some crumpets and they could toast them together in front of the fire. At the gate she paused to look at his window. The curtains were still drawn. She smiled again and turned and walked away.

Soon afterwards Godfrey Thackeray could be observed striding down the street, hatted, mufflered, a stamped envelope in his hand.

Before her mirror Mrs Prendergast swept her hair back, brushing it into a bun. She was dressed in her best tweed suit and today she would powder her face for the first time in years. 'I must look nice, Henry,' she said. 'I have waited so long.'

A bus trundled by, drawing Mrs Prendergast to her window. On the pavement, walking away from the house, the new tenant was carrying a suitcase, hefting it towards the bus stop. A dog trotted happily across the road and followed him, grinning at his heels and sniffing his case. In the distance a telephone bell began to ring. The young man shifted the weight of the case to the other hand and the dog skipped about in surprise.

'Excuse me,' said Mrs Prendergast, struggling to open her window. 'Excuse me,' she called feebly from her second floor window, leaning out. 'Hey!'

He walked on, unhearing, his suitcase slapping heavily against his leg.

'No!' cried Mrs Prendergast. 'You can't leave now. Where are you going? Not now.'

From its perch across the road the parrot eyed her unblinking. Far down the street an old woman shuffled towards her, bent over a basket of shopping. The dog darted into the street and savaged an empty cigarette packet.

Mrs Prendergast leaned weakly against the window sill, panting. The dog stopped, standing in the road and watching him as he disappeared from view. In the distance the telephone bell rang on, unanswered. The dog turned and ambled back, investigating the gutter.